Praise for MJ Fredrick's
Breaking Daylight

"I couldn't put this story down. The writing is stellar, the characters are fantastic, and the plot keeps you on your toes. Anytime you find a book that clutches your heart, makes you tear up, and doesn't let go, you know you've found a winner. Make sure you put Breaking Daylight on your TBR list (I would recommend you purchase it right now to avoid missing out), you won't regret it."

~ *Long and Short Reviews*

"Breaking Daylight is a very nicely done story of murder, suspense, and more. I really was impressed at how much was put `into the telling of this tale by M. J. Fredrick. ...I am looking forward to reading more. ...I am hoping that M. J. Fredrick turns this into a series, hint."

~ *Literary Nymphs*

Look for these titles by
MJ Fredrick

Now Available:

Hot Shot
Beneath the Surface

Breaking Daylight

MJ Fredrick

A SAMHAIN PUBLISHING, LTD. publication.

Samhain Publishing, Ltd.
577 Mulberry Street, Suite 1520
Macon, GA 31201
www.samhainpublishing.com

Breaking Daylight
Copyright © 2010 by MJ Fredrick
Print ISBN: 978-1-60504-908-3
Digital ISBN: 978-1-60504-869-7

Editing by Anne Scott
Cover by Angie Waters

First Samhain Publishing, Ltd. electronic publication: January 2010
First Samhain Publishing, Ltd. print publication: November 2010

Dedication

For Sarah Salazar, who gave me Alex's backstory, and Eleuterio Gonzales, who turns damaged young people into heroes.

Chapter One

"Join the army, see the world," Master Sergeant Alex Shepard mocked under his breath.

He hated jungles. Yet here he was, stuck in another one. Central America this time. Why couldn't he be sent to the Arctic or Siberia? What drew the bad guys to the heat and humidity? Or did the atmosphere make them the bad guys in the first place?

He wiped sweat from his eyes with a shrug of his shoulder. Almost midnight and hotter than midday back home in Texas.

He and his team of Rangers joined a group of DEA agents crouched on a hillside, surveilling a sprawling home in a manmade clearing in the middle of the jungle, a compound as out of the way as Santiago Saldana could make it.

Saldana was the baddest of the bad when it came to drug kingpins. He'd kidnapped, tortured and killed DEA agents, and used the scum-of-the-earth MS-13 gang to get his product over the border. A DEA agent had infiltrated Saldana's inner circle, but hadn't been heard from in weeks, so here they were.

Problem was, they might be too late. They hadn't been able to confirm Saldana's presence in the compound. After three days, there was no sight of him, or the American infiltrator who had been their source of information.

So they waited. In the heat. With the bugs. And the rain.

"Showtime," Sergeant Julian Cervantes murmured from Alex's left, his binoculars trained on the compound.

A light flickered on in the house below and a goddess stepped into the bathroom, a goddess with dark wavy hair, eyes that tilted up in the corners like a cat's, and creamy skin that glowed in the soft light. Alex didn't have to raise his own binoculars to know—they'd managed to be on this side of the compound the past two nights at this time. The side on the hill, with the view of the bathroom which held the luxurious large tub and glassed-in shower.

The goddess wore a silky white robe tonight and flipped back the sleeves as she reached over to turn on the water. She poured in a pink glob of some stuff she'd had sitting on the side of the tub, no doubt sweet smelling, and it foamed under the stream of water. Then she twisted her shoulder-length hair up and pinned it with a clip, exposing a long, graceful neck.

Yeah, he was watching through his binoculars now. This job had damn few perks and she was just about the best he'd seen during his twelve years in.

Then facing the window—she had to think she was alone, with this damn jungle all around—she let the robe slide down her arms in a slow, sensuous movement.

Beside him, Julian uttered what sounded like a prayer.

She was a fantasy woman, with full, round dark-tipped breasts, her nipples erect from the friction of the silk. Her skin was flawless. He could almost feel the smoothness of it under his rough palm, and he folded his fingers against the sensation. The curls at the apex of her thighs were dark and neat.

She stepped into the tub—hell, even her feet were graceful—and slipped beneath the bubbles.

This time Julian swore.

She lathered up some fluffy cloth and smoothed it over her

arm, leaving tiny bubbles in its wake.

The sight of a woman indulging in a bubble bath in the middle of the jungle was so incongruous. She poured soap on the thick cloth, lifted her legs from the bubbles to smooth it on, such feminine actions. So out of place in his world.

Then her hands disappeared under the water. For a while.

She closed her eyes, scooted lower and her lips parted.

"Jesus," Alex breathed.

"I hate bubbles," Julian said in a choked voice.

Alex shouldn't be watching. He should tear his gaze away as she tilted her head back, offering her throat to her invisible lover. Who was she imagining over her, touching her? Saldana? The thought almost gave him the strength to turn away before she reached out of the tub and picked up a bright pink object.

He recognized it from last night, when there had been no bubbles, only the woman, standing with her robe parted, one leg on the edge of the tub and—

"Is that her—?" Julian didn't say the word. "Are those things waterproof?"

She arched her back, revealing soapy breasts. Alex imagined his own touch smoothing away the bubbles to make way for his mouth. Her body undulated with pleasure, sending water and bubbles over the side of the tub.

He jerked his gaze away with a curse. He had no business watching this woman, Saldana's lover, not when he had sweet Rebecca waiting for him back home.

Rebecca, who he'd never seen naked, never touched, never more than kissed. She wasn't ready for a physical relationship after her bastard of a husband had taken off on her, and Alex treasured her too much to push for it. Rebecca Kelso was his ideal, not the goddess in the tub. Rebecca was the kind of woman who would make him sane again after the things he'd seen and done. She would give him balance.

He reached over and smacked Julian's arm. The younger man turned with glazed eyes and inclined his head. The goddess was rising from the tub now, soap bubbles sliding down her flushed body, her movements languid with the aftereffects of her ministrations. The cat eyes were heavy lidded, the look of a satisfied woman.

Alex hadn't seen that look in a long time.

"Let's get out of here," he mouthed to Julian.

"Who is she, do you suppose?" Julian whispered as they slipped through the foliage on their way back to the rudimentary camp. "Saldana's girlfriend? We don't have any intel on a girlfriend."

"Who cares?" Alex said. "She has to know what kind of person he is, and she doesn't care. If that's what floats her boat, she ain't worth fantasizing about."

"Were you not watching the same thing I was? Damn, have you ever seen a woman do that? I've never seen a woman do that."

Alex didn't think Julian expected an answer. Thank God. "She's given up her soul for the lifestyle he offers her."

Julian frowned. "Way out here? Not a lot of women would go for that. The question is, why would he leave a woman like that out here alone so long? Something's wrong with that picture. You don't think he's already moved to the States?"

Alex shook his head. He didn't know. He had to hope they weren't too late. "Maybe there's a leak. The agent who gave us the intel on Saldana also could have given him the heads-up that we were coming. Maybe he tortured it out of him. No matter how, Saldana isn't here. We're wasting time and resources waiting for him to come back."

He pulled away from Julian, as they entered the camp, already reaching in his rucksack for the spiral he kept there. When the younger man went to make a report to Keith Vasquez, the agent in charge, Alex dropped against a tree and flipped open the battered spiral to write to Rebecca.

But he couldn't get his mind off the raven-haired goddess. He had to do something.

"We're wasting time." Alex confronted Vasquez when he couldn't calm down enough to finish his letter to Rebecca. They weren't going to complete the mission by waiting Saldana out. The man was long gone. "Saldana isn't coming back. He's not stupid enough to just drive past us to get home. We missed him. Time to regroup."

"Master Sergeant," Vasquez said coolly, keeping his voice low to avoid detection. "He left something valuable behind."

"What would that be?"

"The woman. Isabella Canales. She's an American citizen."

"Saldana's whore," Alex spat.

Even Vasquez drew back. "You know her?"

"We saw her on surveillance. You think she's worth his freedom? More importantly, does he?"

"Hell yeah," Julian murmured.

Alex shot him a look. "You don't get it. Women like that are a dime a dozen. It's not like he loves her for her mind."

"Maybe not. But she is an American citizen," Vasquez said.

"Who shares her bed with the scum of the earth."

Vasquez tightened his jaw. "One more day. We haven't seen Agent Cortez yet."

They wouldn't. If Saldana was gone, he wouldn't have left his associates behind. If he'd knocked the agent off as a spy, well, they'd likely stumble over his body in the jungle. But this wasn't Alex's call. Vasquez made it clear his opinion didn't count.

"Send me back down to watch, then. Let's make the most of these twenty-four hours."

"I already have Lee and Jordan out there."

"Another man can give you another angle."

"I need you fresh."

Alex looked at him pityingly. "I'm a Ranger. I do what needs to be done." He turned to find Julian.

"You know she's asleep, right?" Alex asked Julian a few moments later as they hiked the short distance to the compound.

"Yeah, but if you think I'm going to be the only Ranger snoozing while the rest of you are on the mission, you got another think coming."

"Did it sound to you like Vasquez wants to go in for the girl?"

"That is what it sounded like."

"He better have damn good information on the inside of that place. I do not want to be booby-trapped in the jungle."

They moved clockwise around the perimeter, west of where they had been at their earlier post. A spider the size of a tennis ball dropped on Alex's arm, and even after he flicked it away, he could feel the hairy legs on his skin.

He hated the jungle.

"What the hell is that?" Julian muttered, directing Alex's attention to a corner of the compound and the slight figure emerging from it.

"A kid?" Alex theorized. "Out for an adventure?"

"In the jungle?" Julian scoffed. "At night?"

"They aren't always smart." Damned if he didn't know that from experience.

"This one is." Julian motioned to the way the figure glanced over his shoulder. "Doesn't want to get caught."

"Running away from a parent."

"You see anyone besides the girl and the guards in there since we've been watching?"

"Christ." Alex focused his binoculars on the kid, only it wasn't a kid. Dark hair was hidden under a dark cap, pulled back into a ponytail that curled in at the nape of a slim, graceful neck. When she turned to look behind her, he saw the feminine tilt of her nose. "What the hell is she doing?"

"Who is it?"

Alex lowered his binoculars and started moving down the hill. "The goddess."

"Who?" Julian asked from behind him. "Where are you going?"

"Vasquez says she's the only thing Saldana cares about, the only thing that will draw him out. We need to get her."

Isabella Canales's heart pounded. Maybe this wasn't the best idea. How would she find the American soldiers in the jungle at night? Clearly they didn't want anyone to know they were here. If that was the case, how would she, with no training and no real jungle experience, find them?

When Eric Reyes had told her soldiers were on their way to take Santiago into custody, she'd hatched her plan. But Santiago had seen the American talking to her, alone, secretively, and he'd gone into a rage. She didn't want to remember what he'd done to the man.

She didn't want to think about what Santiago had done to

15

her. So she'd planned her escape.

She'd staged her show every night at midnight, luring the guards into an unofficial schedule. They would stop outside her window at that time, then they'd move on, leaving her a window of time to get out of the compound unseen. No one would miss her till the morning.

If Santiago even dreamed she was thinking about escaping, her life would be so much worse. She couldn't afford for him to catch her. She couldn't be his prisoner anymore.

Her stolen boots rubbed with every step despite three pair of socks, and the rough fabric chafed her skin after years of wearing only the finest fabrics. She hoped the soldiers had transportation, and that it wasn't far. She hoped she could charm them into taking her home. She didn't want to play her trump card yet.

A stealthy rustling to her left froze her in her tracks. Jaguars were nocturnal, right? But surely they'd be intimidated by her size.

If she were a hundred pounds heavier.

Too late, she realized the jungle had gone silent, as if the creatures in the trees froze as well, hoping the predator would ignore their existence.

Great. She was out in the jungle, in danger of either being discovered by Santiago's guards or being eaten.

Then a face emerged from the brush, only it wasn't the face she was expecting. It was...green and black streaked, and a moment passed before her terror-stricken brain processed it as human, beneath a helmet wound with vines.

A soldier.

Her relief was short lived, because the soldier had an automatic weapon pointed at her chest.

"Isabella Canales?" His American accent skipped over the nuances of her Spanish name.

"Yes?" Her voice was shaky.

"Toss your pack over there and put your hands in the air."

Goddamn. Up close she was even more stunning, a tiny little thing, the kind of woman a man wanted to care for, protect. The kind who, while he was watching her back, stabbed a knife in his.

"You stay there while Cervantes goes through your pack, then he's going to pat you down." He wished he didn't have to hold a gun on her so he could do it himself. To make sure she was safe before he brought her back into camp. That was why.

His grip tightened. Yeah, right.

He glanced over to see Julian unzip her pack and swear.

Alarm raced through Alex, and he weighed possibilities and solutions. Was she armed? Wired? He scanned the area for cover. "What?"

"It glows in the dark." Julian gingerly lifted a familiar pink object from the bag with two fingers.

"Christ." Alex turned back to the goddess. "You're going out into the jungle to get off? Putting on a show in front of a window wasn't enough?"

She didn't answer, every line in her body tight as Julian dug through her things. Keeping one eye on her, Alex noticed Julian paw past a colorful piece of fabric, saw the flash of high heels. Where the hell did this woman think she was going?

"Clean," Julian pronounced after another minute. "You want me to search her?"

"I'll do it." Instead of shouldering his gun, he passed it to Julian, never taking his gaze off her.

He reached to remove her hat, forking his fingers through her hair, dragging the rubber band free, ignoring the silky strands catching on his rough fingers and the flowery scent rising as he dragged his fingers along her scalp. She looked up at him, eyes large and wary, her gaze not leaving him as he moved his touch down her slender back and into the waistband of her cargo pants, skimming his palms over silky panties. The pants were loose enough that he could reach her thighs, but that would mean bringing her body even closer to his. Already he could smell her on his clothes, no doubt the scent from that pink stuff she'd poured in the tub.

Stepping back, he snatched his hands out of her pants. The expression in her eyes was daring. A thrill of admiration ran through him.

He squashed it like the spider.

He reached under her tank top, over her smooth flat stomach, under the underwire of her bra, his fingertips brushing the plump undersides of her breasts.

Soft.

Then hard. Her nipples pebbled at his touch and he tried to quell the lust that rose up. He didn't linger, but searched under her bra, beneath her arms.

Still she looked at him with those dark eyes.

Then he slid his hands down inside the front of her pants, kicking her feet apart.

The flesh of her belly jumped under his palm, but other than that she didn't move when he reached down the front of her panties, over those neat dark curls that he could see in his memory. He probed her heat briefly, businesslike, ignoring the tightening in his groin, then removed his touch to pat down her thighs.

"Take off your boots."

"May I sit?" A thread of fury underlay her voice.

"Be my guest."

She dropped to the ground, untied one boot and shoved it at him. He inspected it, marveling at the large size, then dropped it to the ground beside her and took her other boot.

"What exactly did you think I'd be hiding?" she asked as she retied her boots and got to her feet.

Her voice was too loud, so he hushed her, leaned close to answer. "I've seen women stick some nasty things in some nasty places to kill soldiers."

"You think I'm coming to attack you?" She glared, and her words whipped out. "I'm coming to you for help."

He eased back, the scent of her overwhelming the scent of the jungle and his own stink. "We're to believe you because you tell us? You're not exactly trustworthy."

"Why not?"

He inclined his head toward the compound. "The company you keep." He motioned her to walk ahead of him back to camp. What the hell was she doing out here in the first place? He squelched his curiosity. He was the muscle, not the detective. He'd let Vasquez take care of it. The more distance he kept from Isabella Canales, the better.

But he could still smell her on his hands.

This was a bad idea. Isabella's skin hadn't stopped crawling since the silent soldier had stopped touching her. She was a prisoner, a suspect. She hadn't foreseen this, the disdain, the suspicion. The near-hatred.

The man the soldiers took her to introduced himself as Vasquez and looked down at her like he had found some prize. Her whole body tightened so much she thought her muscles would snap.

"Where is Saldana?" Vasquez asked, his voice smooth.

Isabella didn't fall for the attempt at charm. "You think he'd tell me?"

Vasquez lifted an eyebrow. "You're his lover, aren't you?"

She felt herself flush. The young Hispanic soldier who had gone through her pack studied her, and the others didn't hide their smirks. Only the silent one, the one who had searched her, had no expression. But he watched her.

"He left when he heard you were coming."

"Where did he hear it?"

She swallowed her fear. If they hated her this much now, how would they feel about her if they knew an American had been tortured and killed in the compound and she had been the reason? "I don't know."

"You're lying."

She recognized the tone. Santiago used it often enough to intimidate her. "Why would I lie to you? I need your help."

Vasquez drew back a little. "You need our help?"

She didn't look away, though she wanted to. God, she hated how he was looking down his nose at her. "I want to go home."

"Saldana wouldn't take you?"

She had to turn her head then. "I served him better here. And I didn't have money to leave on my own. You're my only chance."

"You're saying you're his prisoner." The silent soldier spoke at last, and all the contempt she'd gotten from Vasquez was nothing compared to the tone of his deep voice.

"I haven't been allowed to leave the compound in four

years."

"In my experience, hostages don't get silk robes and vibrators."

She kept her head turned away. Of course he'd assume she was lying, but she was still humiliated by the search. "Those things were for his pleasure, not mine."

"Not from what I saw tonight."

She whipped around on him then, needing to release the tension that threatened to shatter her. "You have no right to accuse me. You don't know what I've endured."

"I know drug dealers. I know what whores endure." He pushed away from the tree at last, looking down at her with hate in his dark eyes. A contempt even Santiago didn't show.

"Shepard, that's enough." Vasquez's voice was calm but firm, and the soldier stepped back.

Shepard. That was the name of the man who'd touched her so roughly. He straightened at the order but didn't look away. So she didn't either.

"If you won't tell us where Saldana has gone, we use you as bait," Vasquez said, drawing her attention.

That forced a laugh from her. "You overestimate my value. If I was so valuable, do you think he would have left me here?"

Vasquez moved closer. "I don't believe I do. I know Saldana—I know he doesn't tolerate having something he owns being taken from him."

So, in four years, she had made no gains. She was nothing more than a pawn. Her safety, her happiness was important to no one, and the only person who loved her was thousands of miles away.

She had to get to him.

These men, the three agents and four soldiers, planned on

MJ Fredrick

using her. She would use them in return. She just couldn't let them know.

Surrounded by DEA agents in a Humvee, heading back home, and still Isabella didn't feel safe. Would she ever feel safe again? She would spend the rest of her life waiting for Santiago to catch up to her. What Vasquez had said about him was right. He didn't like things taken from him, and she was his property. If she didn't get back to the States before he found out she was missing, he knew just how to hurt her most. She hadn't thought that part through.

Maybe this wasn't the best plan, but it was the only one she had.

At least the silent soldier, Shepard, was in the other vehicle. She was operating on the last reserves of the courage that had brought her out of the compound, and didn't need his constant judgment.

The ground shook and the men in the front seat swore. There was a rattling, and the man beside her grabbed the back of her head and shoved her down behind the seat onto his lap. She tensed instinctively. This had been a risk, but here? Now?

"Don't fight me."

What did he mean? Did he think she would do what he wanted here?

"They're shooting at—" He grunted, but as soon as she heard the word *shooting*, she was down. The rattling sound was louder, almost constant, sometimes in harmony. God, how many were shooting at them?

The vehicle lurched forward, the front end dropping at an angle, flinging Isabella against the back of the front seat and pushing the other man on top of her.

The shouting in the front seat had stopped, and the man on her made no effort to get off of her, his dead weight pushing her to the floor, bending her waist at a painful angle, something wet soaking into the back of her shirt.

Dead weight. Wet and warm, a coppery scent of...

Oh, God.

She gagged, then forced the thought away and gathered her strength to push out from underneath him. He must weigh over two hundred pounds. She couldn't get enough leverage with her legs to lift him off her, so she had to squirm toward the door sliding out from underneath him.

She reached for the door and the metal handle was hot. She snatched her hand back. God, the car was on fire. She was going to die here, burn alive. Would she never get home, never see—?

"Come *on*."

She turned to the other door, saw a hand reaching in and followed the arm to the dark eyes of Shepard.

"Come *on*," he said, sharper this time.

"I *can't*. He's—" The weight of the man still pinned her to the seat. But the other door was beneath her. "Can you open this door?"

"No."

The heat was unbearable through her pants, and Shepard withdrew his arm, probably figuring she wasn't worth saving. She didn't want to burn to death. She shoved harder against the dead man on her back, and suddenly the weight was gone, she was free, and Shepard was stretching toward her again.

She reached for him, and the truck lurched forward, putting another foot between her hand and his. It felt like she was standing on the door she'd been trying to escape from.

Another lurch, another few inches. She screamed his name and saw him throw himself forward, his fingertips brushing hers.

"You have...to climb...on him," he grunted, every word an effort.

Oh God. Climb on a dead man to lever herself out. Could she do it?

"*Now*. The truck's about to go."

Go where? She wanted to ask, but the strained expression on his face told her now wasn't the time for questions. She put one booted foot on the man lying against the door, then the other, sinking into the soft tissue. Heaven forgive her.

He grasped her wrists firmly, and when she looked up into his eyes, she saw the first hint of approval.

But when he started to lift her—she could see the strain in his face, his arms—she remembered. She couldn't leave her pack behind, not after what she'd risked to get out. She pulled one hand free and twisted to look for it, found it wedged between the dead man and the floorboard.

She pulled her other arm free and bent to tug it loose.

Above her, Shepard swore a string. "What are you doing? Do you want to die? The truck is going over."

She tugged it by the straps and the truck lurched, along with her heart. Another tug and it was free. She looped it over her arm and turned back to see Shepard still waiting, reaching, and she lifted her arms to him.

He pulled both wrists, making her arms ache as the slender bones held the weight of her body. He slid one hand down to her elbow, then the other to her shoulder as her feet scrabbled for purchase first on the seat, finding a place on the back of the front seat, pushing her way toward him. The truck shifted. Over the sound of her pounding heart, she heard the groan of metal, the rattle of more gunfire, which had grown louder now, closer.

Finally Shepard had her, his arms hooked under both shoulders, her face pressed to his sweaty, stubbled throat as he lifted, as the truck fell away in a screech of metal and she tumbled onto Shepard's chest.

She couldn't even catch her breath because he was yanking her to her feet and shoving her—his hand on her ass and back, keeping her bent over as she moved—shoving her toward the sound of the gunfire, the intermittent muzzle flashes. She hesitated, turned to protest, and he tackled her, sending her face first down a muddy incline with a mouthful of vegetation. He skidded beside her on his back, gun cradled to his chest. When she turned to give him a dirty look, she saw that the shooting was coming from the other soldiers, providing cover.

So Shepard could save her butt.

She opened her mouth to say thank you and spit out some leaves.

Shepard turned to her, his eyes hard with a layer of desperation sheening them. "Put your arms around me."

"What?" She fought to focus, still shaking.

"We've got to go down there." He pointed.

She turned. In the moonlight, she could see that a few feet away, the ground dropped off. A cliff.

Shepard was pulling her toward it. She dug her heels in and clutched her pack to her with both arms.

"Are you crazy?" she shouted over the continuing sound of gunfire, both from their enemies and from the other soldiers.

He glared, jaw set, lips tight. "If you don't we are going to die. I don't think you can make it down on your own. Put your arms around me."

She couldn't. She couldn't even look down.

Shepard stuck his face in hers. "Would you rather go back with him?"

That riveted her. She slipped the knapsack against her chest and wrapped her arms around his shoulders. He pulled her against him, harder than she expected, knocking her breath out.

"Don't let go," he said, his muscles bunching so she could feel the tension running through his body as he stepped back, and the world dropped out from beneath her.

Chapter Two

Isabella didn't even have the breath to scream so she tucked her face into his neck, slick and muscular and straining as he held both of them in midair. She was terrified to even look to see how he was holding them. The earth bumped against her back, hard, knocking her breath loose, and with it, a small scream.

"Oh God," she had breath enough to whimper when they dropped in what felt like a freefall.

"Look, I need my other arm to hold us up. You have to hold on to me."

His voice was tight with strain. She felt the vibration of his voice in his throat, could feel his gasps of air in-between the words.

Nausea choked her as they dangled over God-knew-what, and she made a small sound.

"Goddess," he snapped.

The word pulsed through him, beneath the effort of holding up both their weights. "Okay," she whispered.

"Wrap your legs around me for a better anchor."

That was easier said than done with gravity pulling at her feet, and her movement had them swinging. Shepard grunted with the effort to hold them up, and they slid down several feet.

He hissed in pain. Had he ripped up his hand?

"Here." He managed to turn them so that he was between her and the cliff. "Climb the mountain."

It took her a minute to figure out he meant her to walk up the side of the cliff with her legs on either side of his body and wrap her legs around him.

Her stolen boots skidded on the loose soil, and one of her steps slipped, sending them both swaying backwards, in midair, jerking a curse from his lips.

Then she was plastered against him, still not looking.

"I'm letting go now," he said.

She barely had time to tighten her arms around him before he released her. Her ability to cling to him was the only thing keeping her from death.

Her stomach churned. She was pretty sure Shepard wouldn't appreciate her vomiting down his shirt.

He turned so her back was to the mountain again, his feet on either side of her hips, his arms on either side of her shoulders, walking them down. She felt each labored breath, felt the sweat that soaked his collar, smelled his fear.

That did not make her feel better.

"Is there—can I help?"

He let out a puff of breath between his teeth. "No."

"Are the others—?"

"They're coming."

The strain in his voice terrified her. "Shepard—"

"Shut up. Goddess, if you don't mind."

If Alex thought she could do it, he'd get her to turn around, grab on to the vines he was using to climb down the cliff side. But she was already trembling like a leaf and about to choke him, she was holding on so tightly. Her breath came fast and terrified against his throat.

"I see a ledge," he said. "Down and to my left."

"Okay."

If he had gloves on, he would slide the distance, but his left palm was already raw from the uncontrolled slides earlier. So he continued climbing down, ignoring the strain in his shoulders.

He reached with his left foot and pulled them sideways. He needed to release the vine he was on, then find another to get them closer to the ledge. Which meant he had to let go with one hand.

Sucking in a breath, he tightened his grip with his good right hand before reaching out with his left.

He missed and the motion sent them swinging, bouncing off the cliff and dropping another two yards before he was able to brake them by dragging his feet against the wall.

When his breathing evened out, he heard panicked little whimpers against his throat.

"It's okay, it's okay," he murmured, and he scanned to find they were almost even with the ledge. Almost in reach.

He took a step, and then another until he felt the strain on the vine he was holding. Bracing both feet against the mountain, he reached again and grabbed. Wrapping his grip around the new vine, he tested its strength before pulling their combined weight over to it.

He managed two more transfers before his boot touched the ledge, and he used the momentum to pull them both onto it. With his last energy he turned onto his back, cushioning her as she fell on top of him.

She didn't let go, didn't lift her head from his neck. He

rolled so her back was to the cliff, so she was secure, so she wouldn't get hit by any bullets should Saldana's men follow.

When his arms stopped shaking from the strain, he dislodged her death grip on his neck. She unwrapped her legs from his hips, but didn't open her eyes, and clutched her pack to her chest, like she had to hold on to something.

"I bet you're no fun on roller coasters," he muttered, sitting up and resting his forearms on his knees. The ledge they'd landed on was about the size of a twin bed, and God knew how far from the forest floor. He looked at his hands, ripped up from the rough vines he'd descended. The moonlight dimmed and he glanced up to see clouds rolling in over the stars. It wasn't called a rainforest for nothing.

They were screwed.

"Roller coasters have metal bars to hold you in. And tracks. And maintenance workers who check it every day. It's not the same as dangling off a cliff because people are shooting at you."

"What?" He edged back against the cliff beside her and pulled his pack in front of him. He wasn't wild about heights, either, truth be told. He just knew what he had to do and he did it.

"Roller coasters."

She did open her eyes then and looked at him. More specifically, his bloody palms.

"Good Lord, Shepard. What did you do?"

He wouldn't dignify that with an answer, instead opened his pack for his antibiotic cream and gauze. Infection in the jungle was bad news.

"Let me do it," she said, once the first aid stuff was in his lap. "It'll give me something to think about besides how we're going to get down from here."

She took his left hand, closer to her, reached in his pack for his water, and splashed a bit on his palm before dabbing it dry with the hem of her shirt. He could feel the heat of her body when she lifted the shirt. Just inches away would be smooth skin. Soft hands pampered his. He could imagine them on his chest, on his stomach, on his—

Soft because she was spoiled. Because she was the whore of a drug lord. Her luxuries came at the cost of other people's lives. He knew that too well.

He wanted to pull away, but didn't want to give her that much power. She might as well make herself useful.

"Where are the others?" she asked.

"They should be coming along soon. We were first over the cliff. They were covering us, remember?"

He hoped to hell they'd made it over the cliff. He couldn't get back up to them, not with these hands.

"Can you get them on the radio?"

He snorted. "You think they'll be free to answer me? We just have to give them some time."

"How much farther to the ground?"

"Don't know till the sun comes up or we get down there."

"Do you think there will be vines all the way down?"

"I've got a hundred feet of rope in my pack. We'll anchor it here and ride it down. I may even be able to rig a harness."

"With these injuries?" She smoothed the antibiotic cream on his palm, gently, thoroughly. Sweetly.

He pulled away. "We can manage. You may have to haul your own weight."

She lifted huge eyes to him. "What?"

"I have gloves in my pack, and I'll help you, but I can't

carry you down."

She sniffed. "They're just going to have to find my skeleton up here, then, because I can't do it."

He shifted to put more space between them, as much as he dared. "No skin off my nose."

"I thought you needed me to get to Santiago."

He rubbed the edge of his thumb between his eyes. "Yeah, well, we'll find another way."

"I can't do it." Her voice grew shriller. "I am not athletic at all."

"Whatever you say, Goddess. This pack is about seventy pounds without the rope. I'm not hauling another hundred and thirty pounds down."

"I am not a hundred and thirty pounds."

"Whatever. Your choice. You need to decide before the rain starts and makes the rope slippery as hell."

"This isn't my fault, you know." She wasn't as gentle when she wrapped his hand in layers of gauze. "Do you have scissors or something?"

He fished his pocketknife out with a flick, offering it to her blade first. "What?"

"I timed it so they wouldn't miss me till morning. It's not my fault those men are dead."

He didn't say anything. Isabella waited for absolution. But she was asking the wrong person to bestow it. Why couldn't the nice young Hispanic soldier have been the one to save her? He seemed so much more sympathetic. This one was tight with suspicion.

She sawed through the bandage and tucked it into the rest of the gauze, then reached for his other hand. It was pretty raw, with loose strips of bloody flesh. Of course he wouldn't be able to carry her down. But could she make it?

"Sergeant?"

The voice crackling over the radio made them both jump. He fumbled for the radio.

"Yeah, Cervantes, where you at?"

"Where you left me, man. Tangos are history. Get back on up here."

"Everyone okay?"

"We lost the agents in the first truck, and Lee was hit by some shrapnel when the truck blew. Jordan's got him patched up. Get back on up here."

"Can't. We're pretty far down. We slid. Look, we'll meet you at the extraction point."

Isabella quailed at that. He was sending the others away? She would be alone in the jungle with this man?

"We'll come down there."

"Too dangerous. Just meet us."

"Our vehicle was shot to shit. We're on foot."

"Yeah, all right. Try to reach command and see if they can move the extraction closer. Get us a little more time, since we're on foot. Let me know."

He signed off and looked at her. "Get the rope out of my pack and find the gloves."

"Don't you need to rest?" She pulled his pack open wider.

"I'll rest while I make a harness. Not like we have all the time in the world here, Goddess."

"We will if we're dead." She dragged out the rope.

"We'll get to the bottom."

"In one piece?"

He ground his teeth. She could see it in the flexing of his

33

jaw. "Funny how you can trust Saldana with your life and not me."

Safe was not a word she would use to describe how Santiago made her feel, but she didn't think she could convince Shepard of that.

He worked the rope, twisting it into unfathomable knots.

"I thought sailors were the ones who knew all the rope tricks."

He looked up, mouth twisted in a mockery of a smile. "You know a lot of sailors?"

Fine. So he didn't want small talk. "Just one. He was into ropes too."

Shepard's eyebrows jumped and she could have sworn the smile turned real, just for a second, before he turned back to his rope.

"Did you find the gloves?" He lowered the knotted rope to his lap.

She held them out.

He shook his head. "Put them on."

"You need them."

"Your hands are too soft. This rope will rip you up."

"You're injured. You need them more. I can wrap my hands in gauze. That should protect them."

Since that was how he intended to protect himself, he couldn't argue. While she wrapped the gauze around her hands, padding them but still able to close into fists, Shepard muscled a large eyehook into the ledge and threaded the other end of the rope through it. He knotted that end and tested it to make sure it couldn't slide through the eyehook, then dropped the other end off the ledge.

"What are you doing?" She hated the shrill edge in her

voice, but couldn't stop it.

"Making a pulley. Can you stand up?"

She eyed the narrow ledge and her stomach dropped. "God."

"Hold on to the vines there." He motioned to the cliff above the ledge. "I need you to put your legs through this." He held up the harness and she could see the leg holes. Wow.

"Are you sure?" she asked, grabbing the vines before she even stood, using them to pull herself up in the growing light of dawn.

"I'm not going to let you fall." He held the harness so she could put her foot through.

She clutched the vine as she worked up the nerve to lift one foot. "How do I know that? You don't seem to like me very much."

"Doesn't mean I want to see you splat."

"Why don't you like me?" Talking gave her the courage to lift one foot and he slid the rope over her boot.

"Now the other." He tapped the heel of her left boot. "I'd think it would be obvious."

"That you don't like women?" She lifted her foot and stepped through the loop.

He snorted. "I got no problem with women."

"Could have fooled me."

He stood close behind her, so that the only way she could get away was to step toward the cliff. He grabbed her hips and pulled her back. Off balance, she stumbled into him, making him lose his balance. He gripped her harder and threw them both forward. She barely had time to put her hands up to catch herself before she fell face first into the rocky hillside.

"Christ, Goddess. You trying to kill us?" he demanded, his

mouth against her ear.

"I don't—"

"Look, we're in this harness together. We have to be close. Get it?"

She took a deep breath, adjusting to the heat of him, the strength of him against her back. "Got it."

"Just relax."

That was going to happen.

His knees nudged the backs of her thighs when he lifted his feet to slide them through the loops, then pulled the ropes up and snugged them around their butts.

Tying their hips together.

She twisted to look at him when she felt an extra nudge against her butt.

"Are you kidding me?"

He smirked. "I've always been an ass man."

"Leave off the last word and I'll concur."

"Concur—big word for a whore."

She purposely pressed her butt into his groin. "I doubt you'd know what big is."

"Yeah?" He tightened his arm around her waist and stepped backwards.

The air was sucked out of her lungs as they dropped down the side of the cliff. She couldn't even scream as the dirt and vines zipped by. Was he controlling their descent? Could he stop them before they crashed and broke all their bones?

Jesus, Jesus, Jesus. The scream was stuck in her throat as they plummeted down. He wouldn't be able to stop them, not as fast as they were falling, not with his injured hands. She grasped at the rope that whipped past, but snatched her hands back as the rope tore into her bare fingers.

The scent of heated leather hit her—Shepard's gloves on the rope, their only brake. Dust rose up as they hurtled toward the jungle floor—Shepard's boots against the cliff wall as he tried to stop them.

She squeezed her eyes shut against the dirt and rocks he kicked loose, but when she did she saw the view again that she'd seen from the ledge—straight down.

Behind her, over the screaming in her head and her own pounding pulse, she heard Shepard's grunts as he tried to slow them down, his heavy breathing hot against her ear.

With a jerk that snapped her head back into his shoulder and her butt into his groin, they stopped. He lowered his feet, pulling hers with him, and she was stunned to find ground with her toes.

As soon as he loosened the rope from around her hips, she turned around and hit his chest as hard as she could.

"You asshole," she wheezed. "What the hell were you thinking?" She punctuated her question with another smack.

"You didn't like being up there," he said matter-of-factly, though out of breath himself as he peeled off his gloves.

His shredded, bloody gloves.

"You asshole." She pushed him, and he took a step back. "You did it just to scare me, and now look. I hope your hands rot off."

And she bent double and vomited at his feet.

The goddess was trembling, and for a moment, Alex thought she'd drop into the puke at his feet. That was the reason he held on to her arms, not out of any need to comfort her. He just didn't want the smell of puke to follow them through the jungle, attracting animals.

She tilted her head back. Her face was pale in the early-morning light, her lips swollen and dark against her white skin. Her eyes were huge.

"Sorry I scared you," he said, but to break off the apology he released her. She staggered before regaining her footing. "You going to puke again?"

"If I do, I'll have better aim." Her tone was sharp.

He stripped off his ruined gloves and stuffed them into his pocket. "Let's go, then."

With jerky movements, she shifted her pack onto her back and fell into step.

Humidity drenched his skin as they made their way through the dense underbrush. The goddess had trouble keeping up, stumbling along in her boots, unable to keep her footing. No matter what kind of shape her body was in—and there hadn't been an inch he hadn't seen—she panted with exertion.

But she didn't complain. He gave her grudging credit for that. He tried to imagine Rebecca in this same situation, but her idea of an adventure was a picnic in the park. He'd teased her about it, but damn if he didn't wish he was there with her right now.

He wasn't able to reach his men. They were on the mountain, he was in the valley. He sure as hell hadn't expected to be separated from them. They had to find high ground, and soon, if they were to learn the new extraction point.

Only the goddess was really slowing down now. He turned to see her at least five yards back, her face grim and determined.

But damn, five yards. He couldn't keep her safe back there,

and God knew where Saldana's men were. Maybe they thought they'd already killed her, and him with her, but more likely they were looking for her.

Then there were the jungle animals.

"You better get a move on if you don't want to be some animal's breakfast."

Instead of getting scared, she glared through narrowed eyes—a trick, really, given how big and round her eyes were.

"Breakfast, huh? There's a concept."

"Would you rather eat or be shot?" He waited, shifting his weight.

"Ah, the new Terror Diet." She caught up in a few steps, her focus on her feet. "I saw something about it in Entertainment Weekly. If you stop to eat, you die. Based on the movie *Speed*, I think they said."

He scowled. "Can you eat and walk at the same time?"

She rolled her eyes. "I can barely breathe and walk at the same time."

"Good to know your strengths." Nonetheless, he dug an energy bar out of his pack, ripped it open and passed it to her.

She took a bite and her mouth twisted in distaste. Okay, so he'd given her one he didn't like very much to see what she'd do. She didn't disappoint.

"God, it tastes like something you scooped off the forest floor," she said around the mouthful of bar, like she didn't want any part of her mouth to touch it, lest she taste it.

"Sorry. No éclair-flavored energy bars." Sure enough, she'd stopped walking. He backtracked to grab her arm and propel her forward. "But taste isn't the point."

She swallowed gamely—or maybe it was because he yanked her along, and swallowing was just a reflex. But no, she stopped and took another bite.

"Water?" she asked around the mouthful again.

"Finish that first."

"It's like sawdust." Bits of bar flew out of her mouth with her words.

"I can't have you wasting all the water washing it down."

She sniffed. "It's called a rainforest for a reason. In that it rains every day. Water from the sky."

"I have no way to capture it, and no inclination to stop and try. We need to go up and try to get back in contact with the others."

She swallowed again, with more effort. "Up? As in, the mountain?"

"Higher ground, at least."

She looked back the way they'd come. "We left the rope."

"We're not going to climb. There's bound to be a road, an easier way."

"Easier," she repeated, like he'd made a promise. "Okay."

But she didn't move any faster. Hell, even when he turned to help her, she moved like an old lady. Only when he heard her hiss of pain when her foot turned over did he realize what the problem was.

"Where did you get these boots?" He motioned to the footwear that was out of proportion to her body.

"I borrowed them." She swiped the back of her wrist over her forehead. "I didn't have clothes for this."

"Who did you borrow them from?"

He inspected a fallen tree, looking for snakes or anything else that might be using the log as a hiding place. Tossing his pack down, he motioned her to sit. She looked at him warily, then did. He reached for the laces, but she drew her feet back, the quickest he'd seen her move in hours. For the first time he saw that her pants were too big as well, rolled at the hem and at the waist. She was tiny, and these were men's clothes.

"Saldana's clothes?" He squinted up at her.

"No." She folded her arms over the loose waist and dipped her head. "No, if he knew they were missing—"

"Someone you trusted?"

She shook her head. "If he found out someone helped me, it would be terrible for them. I couldn't ask anyone for help."

"Well, you're not asking me." He gripped the heel of her boot in one hand and untied it with the other.

She sucked in her breath when he tugged the boot, and he looked up at her. She was in real pain. This wasn't going to be good.

Blood had soaked through the thick white socks—three pairs, she'd had sense enough for that.

"Jesus." He peeled the socks gently, one at a time, feeling her tense with each layer. If there was this much damage after only walking this morning—the outer sock was little more than a rag—what were her feet going to look like? Hell, he knew. What he didn't know was how he was going to deal with an injured woman in the middle of the jungle with no transportation.

He peeled down the third sock. Her ankle was so small he could wrap his fingers around it. It was ripped to hell, the skin over her Achilles tendon shredded and the flesh over her anklebone where the heel of the boot had rubbed. The tops of her toes—tipped with red nail polish—were raw.

He rested her heel on his thigh, then gave the same attention to the other foot. Only after he dragged his pack over did he look at her face. She had braced her weight on her hands behind her, her whole body tense as she stared at her feet.

"I thought nothing could hurt as bad as stilettos."

That comment surprised a grin out of him. "Yeah, you wouldn't look too great in them now." He pulled out the peroxide, gauze and antibiotic lotion. "You're going to have a hell of a time walking and we've got a long way to go."

She stilled. "You can't leave me here."

He sat back on his heels and sighed. The objective had changed on the mountain—get her back to the States. But how was he going to make that happen when her feet were in this shape and he was on his own? He couldn't protect her and get her out of here. He'd have to stash her until he could do both. "They won't hurt you. We'll get you to the road, they'll find you, take you back."

"To Santiago." Her voice rose in panic. "If he knows I left on my own—"

He dragged a hand over his hair. "You tell him we took you."

She shook her head violently. "He'll know. There's no way you could get in, and I'm forbidden to leave."

"Ever?" He opened a new bottle of water, splashed a bit over each foot, soaking the thigh of his BDUs, and he passed the bottle to her. She took it but didn't drink.

"In four years. I even—" She stopped herself, pressing her lips together.

"Even what?"

She shook her head, her gaze following a trail of ants on the jungle floor.

He cut a strip of gauze, cleaned her wounds with gentle swipes and dabs, applied the antibiotic and started wrapping her foot.

"If you give it an extra layer or whatever I could make it," she said. "It already feels a lot better."

"Your socks are bloody rags." He looked up. "I have to send you back."

"You can't!" She shot forward and grasped his wrist. Her dark eyes were pleading. The kind of eyes that could make a man do anything. He turned his gaze down. "You don't know what he'll do to me."

He pulled his wrist away. "Your choice. You went with him."

She reached for her pack and dragged it close as he wrapped her other foot with less gentleness than the first, needing to get her away from him. But God, how could he make her walk on these feet?

"You're not going to leave me all by myself?"

Damn, she was about to cry.

"We'll find a village. I'm not going to leave you in the middle of the jungle. But even that won't be easy." He held out his hand. "Give me that."

She pulled her pack closer, protective, wary.

"I need to stuff the toes or something so your feet won't have room to slide around."

"I don't have anything."

He tugged the pack free, frowning at her determination to hang on to it. What was she hiding? "I already saw the vibrator. Not that you're likely to be embarrassed by something like that." He unzipped the pack and pulled out a brightly colored silk dress, something fine and expensive, something Rebecca would never wear. No, she liked soft colors and cotton, and had probably never paid more than fifty dollars for a dress. This garment was probably worth four times that, at least.

The goddess whimpered, her gaze focused on it.

He grabbed the garment by the shoulders, took just a moment to imagine how the fabric would mold to her body, and ripped it in two.

You would have thought he'd stabbed her in the heart, the way she cried out and reached for it, trying to pull it from his grasp, too late.

"What the hell?" he demanded, holding it away. "It's a dress."

But the woman who'd refused to cry when she was in a truck on fire, or hanging off the side of a mountain, was sobbing over a dress. Jesus.

He snatched up her boots, one at a time, and shoved the fabric inside, wadding it in the toes. Then he held out each boot expectantly. Lower lip trembling, she took them, eased her sore feet inside and laced them up.

He stood, backing away and grabbing his pack, not taking his gaze off her. Goddamn, he'd never understand women.

She didn't speak as they trudged through the jungle. Pissed about the dress, no doubt. She'd stopped crying, though. She was making an effort to keep up. After seeing the state her feet were in, he knew what an effort that was. He couldn't quite make himself admire her for it, though.

"Are you going to sulk about the dress till we get to the extraction point?"

She didn't respond.

"Saldana bought you that dress? That why you're so upset?"

"You wouldn't understand." Her tone was dull, different

than before.

"I bet. I don't get women who sell their bodies to scum of the earth for pretty things."

That put her back up and her tone sharpened. "I'm not going to explain myself to you."

"Explain this to me." He fell back to walk beside her. "How did you end up in Central America?"

"Studying."

Right. "Studying drug lords? Terrorists?"

She tossed her ponytail, strands of hair coming loose every which way. "Spanish. Immersion."

Shepard turned, incredulous. "Yeah, I hear Saldana has a real thing for linguists."

"I danced to pay my tuition."

She didn't even blush at the admission.

"Stripped, you mean." Why was he surprised? Maybe he was just surprised she was so open about it. And surprised that the image of her in a G-string hanging on a pole came so easily.

Goddammit.

Isabella knew they were approaching a village because the trees cleared out. The path in front of them was wide enough for a vehicle. In fact, she could see wheel ruts. Not a car, but four wheels.

Amazing what you could see on the ground when you didn't have the energy to lift your head.

The pain was constant now, each step sending shocks of it through her system. Each time she lifted her foot, the weight of the boot pulled it downward, rubbing the boot across her raw toes. The insides of the boots were soggy. She didn't think it was from the rain. The wetness only added to the friction.

When she got home, she would only wear flip-flops, no matter how mangled her feet looked.

When she got home. The hope was even farther away now than when she was in the compound. She hadn't thought of all the obstacles to cross in escaping Santiago, in getting out of the country.

Now Sergeant Shepard wanted to leave her in this village so she could go back to Santiago. Clearly he didn't want her blood on his hands.

He'd just as soon leave that responsibility to Santiago, which is what would happen if she went back to him. She'd seen what he was capable of, firsthand.

Ahead of her, Shepard halted, motioning for her to stop as well.

Stopping hurt worse than walking, and she swallowed a whimper.

Okay, maybe not, if the look Shepard shot her was any indication.

They drew back to the trees, Shepard pulling her with him. Her muscles were so stiff, she staggered at the movement.

Her heart thudded as Shepard palmed his pistol and moved forward, his lean body at once taut and graceful as he moved into the village. She'd never seen anyone so focused. But of course their lives depended on that skill.

She wondered what had him worried and hoped he didn't shoot a villager by mistake. He was that tense.

He disappeared, and her pain disappeared as she held her breath, waiting for him to return.

She was alone in the silent jungle. Quiet jungles meant danger. Her legs were water, her boots planted in the mud, as every nerve in her body screamed for her to run after him.

Her muscles finally heeded her nerves and she stumbled in the direction she'd seen Shepard go. She rounded a hut only to be yanked back against a hard body, a large hand over her mouth.

Before panic choked her, she realized the hand was rough and bandaged.

Shepard.

Still, he'd scared the hell out of her. She plowed her elbow into his stomach—his hard stomach—and threw her weight forward but he held fast.

"Hold still." The words brushed against her ear.

It was then she realized they were in the shadows, and that there was no movement in front of them. Over the scent of Shepard's sweat, she smelled something else, more acrid.

Behind her, she felt Shepard working to control his breathing, though she could feel his heart thundering against her back. What had him so uptight? The silence?

Then he eased his hand from her mouth, turning her at the same time so she could see his finger over his lips.

Desperate to know what was going on, she opened her mouth, but she stopped herself before the words came out, his razor-sharp look casting a warning. Once he was sure she would be quiet, he edged her behind him, training his gun from side to side in stiff-armed sweeps.

God, were those—she choked back a cry of despair when she realized—

She must have made some sound because Shepard turned his head infinitesimally in warning. What did it mean that she understood him?

Bodies. God, bodies everywhere. The smell she hadn't been

able to identify was blood. Everywhere.

This time she had to stifle a gag, because now she understood he thought whoever did this might still be there.

She twisted her fingers in the back of his shirt as she moved behind him. To the side, she saw a woman sprawled on her stomach, her back ripped and bloody. Beside her lay a small body.

She turned her head, pressed her face between Shepard's shoulder blades. He stopped, mid-step, his muscles tight. Understanding he couldn't move freely with her plastered against him, she eased away a little. Still, she didn't take her eyes from the back of his neck, where sweat trailed from his neat hairline to the collar of his T-shirt. She stumbled after him, afraid to look at her feet to see what she might be stepping on.

Finally, she felt his tension ease, and he lowered the gun.

"They're gone," he said, keeping his voice low, sounding disappointed. *Disappointed.*

"What happened?" she asked, her own voice rough.

"Automatic weapons." When he turned to look at her, his eyes were hard, flat. That hate again. "Know anyone with automatic weapons in these parts?"

Santiago. "But why?"

"My guess? A message to you, sweetheart. That he won't let you go easily."

"But how does he know where we're going?"

"I don't know." He scrubbed a hand down his face, looking uncertain for the first time since she'd seen him.

That was scarier than his angry, hot eyes.

Which flashed at her as if the moment of weakness had never happened. "But clearly this was a warning, to you, to us, to anyone who might help us."

She staggered a step back. "You think these people are dead because of me?"

"Would Saldana's men be out of the compound if they weren't looking for you?"

Oh God. Her stomach heaved but nothing was left. Still, the bile burned her throat, her mouth, and she turned her head to spit it out, holding her hair back as her body, her soul turned inside out.

Her life for these people. Could she survive knowing that these people had died because of her? She wanted to ask Shepard, but he was looking at her with such disgust.

The same disgust she felt for herself.

Chapter Three

"We have got to go." Alex grasped her arm, but her resistance surprised him. He knew she hurt, but he thought her will to survive was stronger.

He turned. Her gaze was riveted by a kid sprawled on his stomach, arms stretched out toward a woman—his mother?

The goddess stared. Damn, was she going to break down on him? Last thing he needed was a hysterical female.

"We can't just leave them like this," she said through lips that didn't move. "We need to bury them."

He felt sick about it, but said, "Right, and Santiago's men will just hang back and wait for us to finish our good deed. We're moving on."

She dug her heels into the soft earth beside one of the smallest victims. Neither of them looked down. Instead, her eyes burned into his.

"I hate you."

"I'm hurt." He headed off into the jungle, hating himself pretty much as well.

Isabella followed, barely able to see him through the tears of sorrow and anger that blurred her vision. Each step took them from the people who needed their help, and she couldn't forgive him for it.

Finally, she couldn't go any farther. They'd left the village an hour ago, maybe longer. Her muscles were watery and her feet screamed in a symphony of pain. She was dizzy and she was thirsty and she was hot. But she hadn't spoken to Shepard since they'd left the villagers lying in the open, waiting for the jungle to reclaim them.

He hadn't spoken to her, either, had gotten as far as twenty feet away before slowing to wait for her. She'd thought he meant to leave her, like he had the villagers, and part of her was relieved. She couldn't go on much longer.

He was ahead of her again, standing, waiting, every line of his body telegraphing his impatience. She didn't hurry to catch up—couldn't—but when she reached him, he swung his pack to the ground and said, "Break," without looking at her.

Why was he mad? Oh, yes—he thought it was her fault those people were dead.

He might be right. She couldn't care just now.

As he crouched and opened his pack, she swayed on her feet. He pawed through, then reached up toward her with a power bar in his fist. She took it, unwrapped the plastic and scarfed the crumbly bar, barely tasting it, before he stood, unwrapping his own.

His gaze flicked from the empty wrapper, to her, for the first time since the village. "Why didn't you tell me you were hungry?"

Surely he was smart enough to figure it out, so she didn't answer. When he rolled his eyes, she knew he'd made the connection.

"Still mad?"

She didn't have the energy to argue with him about leaving those people, didn't want to tell him about her fears that he'd leave her as well, so she said nothing.

"There was a reason you snuck out of the compound, right?" he asked.

His ability to form complete sentences stunned her. He had to be as exhausted as she was. She merely nodded.

"I figure you probably don't want to go back or end up like those people."

The memories of those people swamped her, choking her, and she shook her head. Her eyes burned. She was going to cry and he was going to hate her even more.

"If we die out here, no one's going to bury us," she whispered.

"No."

Her breathing became faster as she swallowed her tears, then she whirled away from him, too tired to fight them anymore. Dizzy, she dropped to her knees, dug her fingers into the decaying vegetation and stopped resisting.

Terror, rage, sorrow gushed out in a torrent, monsters her body struggled to purge. Behind her, Shepard loomed, making no effort to quiet her, to comfort her, to chide her. He only stood, waited until she got control of herself.

Sitting on her heels, she wiped at her face. She couldn't look at him, at his judgmental eyes. But once her vision cleared she saw the canteen he offered her. She took it silently and drank big gulps, passed it back considerably lighter.

He sighed and capped it. "You need to get some sleep."

If he'd told her they would be airlifted into Air Force One, she wouldn't have been more surprised. Or relieved. But... "Where?"

He pointed up, still looking at her. "There."

She followed his finger. "In the tree."

"Yep."

"How are we going to get there?"

He swung his pack on his shoulder and grinned—the first smile she'd seen, and the flash of white teeth took her breath away. She had thought he was handsome before, sure, the lean planes of his face accented by his shorn brown hair and his body honed to perfection. But there had been nothing in his eyes but contempt.

Until now.

He was challenging her, probably his way of motivating her. A challenge, she could take. Except she'd never climbed a tree before, not even as a kid. She'd always been a princess.

"Why in the tree?" she asked.

"Because if Saldana's men come, they won't be likely to look in the trees."

That made sense. "What about jaguars?"

"They're nocturnal. We have a couple of good hours before we have to worry about them." He followed her gaze up. "It's not the featherbed you're used to, but it will be safe enough. I'll go first." He moved toward the tree and inspected it for a moment, finding hidden footholds before muscling his way to the first fork, about ten feet off the ground.

Then he turned and reached for her.

Right. She secured her pack behind her and gripped the tree, trying to find the footholds he'd found in the slick bark. Her already throbbing feet protested as she clumsily bumped them against the trunk, searching for a way to get up.

"What's the problem?" he asked.

"I'm not as closely related to my ape ancestors as you," she muttered and hauled her weight onto the slight foothold she'd found, only to slide loose and hit the ground with enough force to have her feet screaming.

"Jesus, Goddess."

"I've never climbed a tree before," she said, frustration making her grit her teeth. "And quit calling me that. My name is Isabella."

"I know your name."

She tried again, with a different foothold, refused to see how far away he was.

"I know what yours is too," she said, almost breathless with the effort of hauling herself up almost two feet from the ground. Her stupid pack made her off balance. "That A on your name patch? It's Asshole, isn't it?"

He chuckled softly, but his voice sounded close. She looked up in surprise to find his fingers closer than she thought, and she gave herself a heave until their fingers brushed, another till he could grip her wrist and pull.

When she was sitting beside him in the Y of tree branches, he turned to her and grinned. "You got it, sweetheart."

The first fork in the tree wasn't good enough for him. No, it was too close to the ground. So they had to climb to the next one. If he thought she was going to be able to fall asleep twenty feet from the ground, where one shift of her weight while she was sleeping could send her tumbling out of the tree and onto her head...

"Come over here." It was a command, so she paused. They were in close-enough quarters but he wanted her closer.

Part of her hesitation was that, well, she was a little scared of him. He didn't like her, had no reason to keep her safe, and she was slowing him down. He might well push her to the ground.

The other reason was that she smelled to high heaven, and

she was still woman enough to worry about his reaction to that.

Not that he smelled any better.

Not that she noticed what he smelled like.

"Goddamn." He stopped himself. "Isabella, get over here. Just treat me like your pillow, all right?"

Shepard as a pillow. That would be about as comfortable as a rock. But he would anchor her. Reluctantly, she edged closer so they were hip to hip. He shifted his arm so he could loop it over her shoulders, holding her against his side. She had no choice but to relax back against his shoulder. Hard, just like she thought.

She'd never slept with a man's arms around her, never experienced this level of intimacy. Why did she have to realize that now? She'd never get to sleep.

"How are your hands?" she asked so she wouldn't be focused on the rhythm of his breathing, the rise and fall of his chest that suddenly consumed her field of vision.

"Good. How are your feet?"

Liar. "Peachy."

"I'll check them before we leave." His chest rumbled with the words. "I'd have you take off your shoes right now, but no telling what the blood might attract."

She was definitely not going to get any sleep thinking about that. "How long till we can get in contact with the rest of your crew?"

"I'll try again in the morning. One step at a time, Goddess."

"Okay." His voice, his words, were soothing, along with the steadiness of his heartbeat beneath her cheek. She fell asleep almost immediately.

The goddess was drooling. That was the only explanation

for the wet patch under his nipple, right about where her mouth was.

He'd awakened himself after two hours of sleep. He wanted to be out of the tree before nightfall and he had to rebandage his hands and her feet.

She was so relaxed against him, one hand sprawled across his belly, one leg thrown across his.

And she was drooling. The sleep of the innocent.

He, however, had a hard-on. He thought about putting her palm over his erection, be the asshole she thought he was. But then he'd be just like her. Goddamn her.

Now that he'd found his anger again and let it supplant any tenderness, he could wake her. He shoved at her shoulder.

"Come on, Goddess. Time to get moving."

She didn't move, at first, just made a soft sound of protest that shot to his groin. Christ.

He shoved harder. "Isabella. We have to go."

She curled into herself, dragging her fingers across his stomach, her leg along his.

"Please. A little longer," she said in a husky voice.

"No time." He kept his tone as sharp as necessary to penetrate her sleep. Had he been too soft with her before? Did she think he wasn't in charge here? "Let's go."

She sat up slowly, wiping drool from the corner of her mouth with the shoulder of her shirt. Her face reddened when she saw the wet patch on his shirt. At least she wasn't looking at the bulge in his pants.

"Can you get down by yourself? I have to pee." He pushed her away till no part of her was touching him, then he started down without waiting for her answer.

The jungle was scary as hell at night. The sounds, the cries of the animals that lived there, intensified. Even though she couldn't see all the animals during the day, not being able to see them at night was more frightening.

Shepard wasn't talking again. Had she only imagined his kindness earlier? But no, she hadn't been tired enough to dream something that couldn't have happened, and she'd awakened in his arms, after he'd offered himself as her pillow. She hadn't imagined that. What had happened while she was sleeping?

She hated the silence, though. It left her head too full of her own thoughts and fears. She had to talk, to hear another voice, or go crazy. So she hit upon a topic of conversation.

"Tell me about her," she said.

He whipped his head around. "What?"

"Tell me about your girl. The one who is so much more deserving than I am."

He grunted and continued forward. "I don't want to talk."

"Do we need to be quiet? Are they close?" She eased closer to him, regretting that her temper overcame her sense of survival.

His shoulders relaxed a bit. "I haven't seen any sign."

She fell back, allowing more space between them. "So we can talk."

"I don't want to talk."

"I got that. But I want to know about her. You miss her."

He didn't say anything.

"Where does she live? Where you live? Do you live together?"

He whipped around. "Goddess, as far as I'm concerned, you're the enemy. I'm not telling you anything about my private

57

life."

She shut out the pain that his words caused. "Not that you have one or anything, what with trekking through jungles all over the world."

He stiffened. She didn't know if it was the private-life comment or...

"I hate jungles." He stalked off.

A few hours later—God knew how long they'd been walking, the trees were so thick, it could be broad daylight but they'd never know it—Shepard signaled for her to stop again.

"What?" she whispered, right up behind him, and he glared.

Okay, so she'd be quiet. Except the need to be quiet meant danger. Her heart pounded and she wouldn't have been able to hear him if he did speak to her.

Now what?

"Village," he finally said, so low, she mostly just read his lips.

Her heart filled with dread. If Santiago's men had been here first, she couldn't handle seeing that carnage again.

"Not dead," Shepard said in that less-than whisper.

How did he know? But she allowed herself a small measure of relief at his words.

Then he dropped his pack to the ground and motioned for her to have a seat on a fallen log. "We wait here till dawn."

Alex couldn't make any headway with the chief of the village. He wanted information and he wanted supplies, but either the man didn't understand Alex's admittedly choppy Spanish or he didn't like the fact that an American soldier had been waiting at the edge of his village at daybreak. Not that Alex

Breaking Daylight

could blame him.

The man stood stubbornly despite Alex's bargaining, cajoling, doing damn near everything but begging.

He stomped back to Isabella's side, disgusted.

"What is it you want from him?" she asked wearily.

The woman was so tired she could barely stand, and he couldn't get his mind off her mangled feet. Both issues were in the forefront of his mind as he spoke to the chief, and probably his frustration had mangled his message. "Best case? Transportation. Failing that, some supplies to replenish what we've used. I hadn't counted on hiking two of us out on the supplies I had." He'd given her his last power bar this morning. Hunger didn't improve his mood.

"Okay." She gave him the gun he'd let her carry so he would appear less threatening. She stepped back, bent her head and shook her hair loose. Then she straightened and scooped it back into a ponytail. Smoothing her palms down the front of her filthy T-shirt, she squared her shoulders and sauntered toward the chief.

As best she could on those bad feet, anyway.

While Alex watched, she moved in close to the chief. She tucked a stray dark curl behind her ear, tilted her head one way, her hip another. She smiled, her eyes bright with it, her whole face transforming to something even more beautiful, despite her lack of makeup and her exhaustion. The chief asked her something about being a captive, but she only laughed, letting her head fall back, exposing the line of her throat. Alex was riveted to the sight of her long neck, even ringed as it was with dirt.

The chief was riveted too.

She said something to him and he replied in rapid-fire Spanish. Isabella gave him all her attention, watching him, nodding, touching his arm.

Christ, what a player.

She waved in Alex's direction and the chief nodded. Isabella leaned forward and kissed the man's cheek before she turned and approached Alex with a smirk replacing that gorgeous smile.

"What the hell was that?" he demanded.

"Vicente regrets that he doesn't have enough food to send with us, but we're welcome to join his family for breakfast. Unfortunately, that won't be for a couple of hours, so he said we are more than welcome to use their facilities before breakfast."

"Their facilities," he repeated, beating down his disgust that she was able to charm the man when he wasn't able to reason with him.

"A waterfall," she said, a tinge of rapture in her voice as she pulled her hair free of its ponytail. "It will feel so good to be clean again."

Alex checked out the river before he let Isabella go in. Just what he needed was to pick a bunch of leeches off her naked body. But calling it a waterfall was a little grand. It was no more than a steady flow of water over rocks into a clear pool surrounded by low plants—no place for predators to hide. She was safe enough.

From the moment he said so, she started stripping, and he turned, intending to go into the village.

He stopped at the edge, realizing he had no allies there. Not that it was out of the ordinary—US soldiers weren't welcome many places. He should be relieved not to have to worry about Isabella. He could leave her here. Once he had his supplies, he could haul ass to meet the rest of his team and get the hell out of this country.

Except the DEA wanted Isabella for questioning, and they'd just send him back in for her.

For a drug lord's whore.

Not for the first time, he wished he could see Rebecca, touch her, kiss her, take comfort in her innocence. He loved how calm he felt with her, not the tension he experienced every moment with Bella. Too much time had passed since he'd seen her and he needed the normalcy he felt with her again.

Figuring Isabella must be close to done bathing and needing to make sure she was safe, he headed back to the waterfall.

Isabella stood beneath the flow of water, her profile to him, her arms lifted to thread through her hair as the water pounded her body. She was bare-breasted, wearing only a tiny pair of pink panties. And she was humming.

Christ have mercy, she was the most gorgeous creature he'd ever seen.

She turned, opening her eyes, looking right at him as if she'd felt him watching her. She didn't cover herself, only watched him watch her.

"Are you coming in?" she called at last.

Why the fuck not? He was filthy, sweat dried on his skin beneath layers of more sweat. He was hot and he was horny— the cool water should take care of both those issues.

He sat to unlace his boots, then stuffed his socks in them to prevent any fun surprises like snakes. He stood and stripped down to his skivvies. What the hell—he stripped those off too.

The goddess was staring. Let her look.

He stood and inspected the clear depths, too shallow to dive. So he took two steps back and cannonballed in, drawing his legs up and giving a whoop.

The pool swallowed him, cold and clear, washing away the past two days. His ass hit the bottom hard and he pushed to his feet, letting the water sluice over him. He whipped the droplets out of his face and still the goddess stared.

"Like what you see?" he challenged.

She did. She really did. His body was hard, sculpted, and there was something appealing about the dog tags resting against his bare chest.

The water came to his ribs, but it was so clear she could see down to his— And it was very impressive.

What would it be like to be with a young virile man instead of one who needed tricks to get off?

No, she couldn't even think like that. Shepard served one purpose and one only—to get her home.

Besides, he hated her.

"Aren't you going cover yourself up?" he asked snidely.

"Why?" she asked, determined not to let him make her feel bad about her body. "You interrupted my bath."

"You've been down here half an hour. You should be— pruney."

"I don't want to be hot again. It's not like I'm wasting water."

"Well, you can't trek through the jungle like that."

"Is it time to go already?"

"Soon."

She sat on one of the moss-covered rocks, dangled her toes in the pool. Shepard moved closer, took one of her feet in both hands to inspect it. Blisters swelled across her toes, some of the skin was rubbed raw, especially around the ankles. His expression grew somber.

"How are you walking on these?"

"You're not giving me much choice."

He looked up at her. "Maybe your friend the chief has something, salve or socks or better fitting shoes."

"So that's why you're mad at me now? I was able to accomplish something you weren't because I was nice?"

"You were able to accomplish something I couldn't because you're a beautiful woman. And I was nice." He dropped her foot.

"You don't know what nice is. It was fake and he could tell you were just using him."

"You weren't?"

"Of course. He had something I wanted. People do it all the time. But the point is to make them feel like they're doing it because they want to, not because they're intimidated."

His nostrils flared. He did that a lot when he was angry. "I was being nice."

"Please. You're trained to intimidate, and you're a master at it. I think part of the reason you don't like me is that I talk back." She slipped off the rock and into the pool. He took a step back, but only a step. "Am I right? Don't lie to me."

"I don't like you because you use your body to get what you want."

She wasn't prepared for him to admit that he didn't like her, though she couldn't say why. Shepard had been nothing if not brutally honest.

So she'd be honest too. "I use my body to survive."

"Because taking your clothes off and lying underneath men is the only way to survive? You seem smart enough that you could have found other options. You took the easy way out."

"Trust me when I say nothing about my life has been easy." She gave in to the urge to swim away, to put some distance between them. Honesty hurt.

"You've made your choices. How your life has gone is based on those choices. You don't know what a hard life is unless you don't have choices."

"You're right."

She swept her arms back and forth in the water, treading water, angry at herself that he was making her ashamed of her body. She put her feet down and rose to her full height, gloating when his gaze dropped to her nipples and the water running down her body. His jaw tightened.

"I made bad choices. Coming here, letting myself be dazzled by Santiago. But that doesn't excuse what he did to me, what I had to do to survive it. Yes, I became a whore, but that wasn't the choice. See, Santiago couldn't get it up after a few weeks, so he bought me the vibrators. Watching that excited him for a while, but then it was his guests he wanted to watch fuck me. He had a lot of guests. Old, smelly guests."

Shepard watched her grimly, his eyes giving nothing away. "You could have refused."

"Gee, thanks. That never occurred to me. The first time, I didn't think Santiago would go through with it. It was too late to fight then. The next time, I was beaten—by both of them—until I couldn't walk for days. The last time I tried to fight, he took my son away." She hadn't been ready to share that information, hadn't decided if Shepard even needed to know. But now it was out in the open.

Shock flared on his face, finally an emotion. "You have a son?"

64

Chapter Four

"He's three." Her voice softened as she spoke of her child. "Santiago sent him back to the States, to his family there. That's when I came up with my plan. I have to get back to him before he forgets who I am."

A mother. Christ. Just when he was getting to understand her. Hell, he appreciated her honesty even though her story disgusted him. But to learn she was a mother...

"Saldana's kid?"

Her expression twisted—was that revulsion? She nodded. "His name is Hector."

"Saldana sent him to the States."

"To his family in Miami, he said." She crossed the pool to where her clothes were stretched out on rocks, like she couldn't bear to be naked when she spoke of her son.

"How long ago?"

"Almost four months." She hauled herself out of the water and slipped on the T-shirt, which clung to her wet body. "I didn't know what to do," she added quickly, as if she didn't want him to judge her further. "I had no way to leave. When Eric Reyes told me soldiers were coming, I knew that was my only chance to get away. I never thought it would take days to get to the States. I thought it would be only hours, and Santiago wasn't there, so he wouldn't know I was gone right away. Now, no matter how fast we get to Miami—" She choked back a sob.

"Santiago will have hidden him," Alex concluded.

She looked at him, stricken, as if hoping he wouldn't think so too. "I have to get to him, Shepard. Don't you see?"

He did. Only he knew the DEA would be waiting for her when they got to Tegucigalpa. She'd be debriefed before they let her go. If they let her go. Her kid could be in kindergarten in Timbuktu before she found him.

Part of him wondered if that wasn't for the best. What chance did the kid of a drug lord and a whore have? The only way Alex had survived a similar lineage was through entering the foster system. That alone had saved him from repeating his parents' mistakes.

He wanted to say it to her, the part of him that wanted to punish her. But her eyes were big and sad, and while he told himself she could be acting to gain his sympathy, she knew him well enough by now to know he didn't have any.

He almost wished he did.

"The dress, the one you ripped up, that one was his favorite. He would fall asleep rubbing the fabric between his fingers. I was going to wear it when I found him."

He clamped his jaw against the offer to buy her another one when they were in civilization. After all, what kind of mother wore a dress like that to care for her child?

She didn't look at him, clearly not wanting to feel his judgment. She reached for her socks, brown with blood, ripped by friction and shook them out.

He swam over to her. "Wait. Your feet need to be dry. See if these people have any socks, anything you can wrap your feet in, or you'll get jungle rot."

"Doesn't matter," she murmured.

He grabbed her arms, forcing her to look at him. She let out a little cry of alarm but he didn't release her.

"What good are you going to do that little boy if you're laid up in a hospital somewhere? If you don't take care of yourself, how can you expect to take care of him?"

She lifted her gaze, her lips tight with anger. "I know you can't believe me, but I would do anything for him."

He didn't believe her, but it wouldn't help the situation to say it. "Then do what I say."

The anger dissolved and she nodded, backing away.

"It's not good for you to wear wet underwear, either. You could have some serious chafing."

She climbed to her feet. "I have clean underwear."

She pulled them out of her pack—God help him, white lace ones this time—and stripped off the pink ones. Right in front of him. What the hell? Just when he'd finally got his arousal under control. Jesus Christ.

He couldn't tear his gaze away, even as she stepped into the panties, pulled them up those gorgeous legs and snapped them in place at her hips.

She reached for her pants and looked down at him, knowledge in her eyes. "Breakfast should be almost ready. Are you coming?"

"I'll be right there," he said through his teeth.

Isabella was sitting at the table with her new friend and his family, laughing, eating like a starving person, when Alex joined them. Her smile was bright with mischief when she looked at him.

"Everything all right?" she asked, as if she knew just what

he'd been doing.

He grunted in response and sat at the end of the bench when others made room for him.

"We were gone so long, they thought we were having sex."

He grunted again. She was trying to get a rise from him, and she was, just not one he was going to show her.

"They didn't have any socks, but they gave me some sandals." She held up one foot with a simple leather sandal on it.

"You won't get far in those."

"That's the good news. They've got a truck."

That *was* good news. His mood improved immediately. "How much?"

"Not for sale, but they'll give us a ride into Tegucigalpa. That's where we're heading, right?"

"Right." There would be a third party there to keep him from doing anything else idiotic.

"We leave after breakfast." She beamed at him. "Did I do good?"

"Thank you for not leaving me there," Isabella said softly as she settled in between one of Vicente's burly sons and Alex on the old Ford's bench seat. "I know you wanted to leave me."

"I have orders from the DEA to bring you in," he said.

She sobered. "Of course. Orders."

"How long is it to Tegucigalpa?" he asked Vicente's son.

"Six or seven hours."

Alex sat back, impatient to have this mission accomplished already. To get Isabella Canales out of his hair.

"At least we won't be walking," Isabella said. "You can get

some sleep."

As if he could relax with her all pressed up against him. "Yeah, sleep."

"I suppose it's too much to hope this thing has air conditioning," she continued cheerfully, clueless about what lay ahead. "But I'm going to sleep."

"Knock yourself out." Maybe then he'd be less aware of her.

She closed her eyes and leaned her head back against the seat once Vicente's son started the engine. She shifted, and shifted again, and again.

Her eyes popped open after just a few minutes. "I can't sleep. I'm too excited. Tell me a story."

He snorted, looking out the open window at the passing jungle. "I'm no storyteller."

"I don't want you to make up one. I want you to tell me about your girl. What's her name?"

He turned to look at her. "Rebecca. Why are you so determined to know about her?"

"Because I want to know what kind of woman makes a man like you fall in love."

"A man like me?"

"A hard man. One who sees things in black and white."

"Are you insulting me?"

"Are you denying that's what you do? Is she as righteous as you?"

"Rebecca hasn't seen the bad things in life like I have. She doesn't believe people are all bad. She can't really wrap her mind around why jobs like mine exist."

"She's your pure, like Hector is mine. You don't want this part of your life to touch her."

"Yeah," he said, surprised by her insight.

"She wouldn't judge me."

"Like you said, I wouldn't let her see that side of my life."

She flinched at the words, but she didn't give up. "How did the two of you meet?"

"You're kidding me."

"I read romance novels to go to sleep. Do you have a romance novel in your pack?"

"How I met Rebecca is not a romance novel," he said with a smirk.

"Is it going to have a happily ever after?" she asked.

"Well, yeah, I hope so."

"Then tell me."

"All right. It was at the movies. I'd gone with some buddies. She was there, in line in front of me, so pretty. Real old fashioned, you know? Blonde and wholesome. She was even wearing a skirt." She'd looked like one of those girls out of an old movie, fresh-faced and innocent. She'd been wary of him. His certainty that they belonged together scared her at first. As soon as he knew, he'd backed off, unwilling to risk losing her. His intensity had scared him. He'd never wanted anything as badly as he wanted a future with Rebecca. A nice, normal picket-fence future. "I couldn't take my eyes off her. So I blew off my buddies and went to some chick flick with her."

He turned to see Isabella's reaction but she was asleep, her head back against the seat, her mouth open.

Once she was out, he contacted his team to tell them they would meet back at Tegucigalpa. After he'd made contact, he relaxed. Well, as much as he could with the goddess snuggled against him like he was some goddamn pillow.

For God's sake, he'd been an asshole to her. Why did she

feel comfortable enough with him to curl up practically in his damn lap? Was she just so comfortable with men? He couldn't imagine her being as unguarded with Saldana and his men, but maybe he was mistaken.

The other thought that worked its way into his brain was that the other men in her life were even worse assholes than he was. He knew that was the sympathetic side of his brain talking. He couldn't afford to be sympathetic.

But when he dropped off to sleep, it was Isabella's laughing brown eyes he dreamed of.

Returning to civilization, even the civilization of the city of Tegucigalpa, Honduras, resulted in culture shock after being in the jungle for weeks. Alex could only imagine what it was like for Isabella after four years. He watched her pressed to the grimy glass of the truck windshield, taking in the sights, barely breathing as her attention darted from one thing to another. She was like a little kid. He swore he heard her whimper when they passed a bookstore.

As Vicente's son Gerardo made his way through traffic, Isabella kept up a running stream of comments, reading signs aloud, chattering about the people and the cars, making the jungle seem downright quiet.

Gerardo knew the way to the embassy, thank God, and dropped them off in front, by the concrete rows of planters. Isabella hobbled for a moment on her bad feet, and Alex caught her elbow. As he guided her into the building, he wondered if his men had made it back to town.

Together they approached the marine standing at the entrance. Alex could feel Isabella's tension rising with each step. He couldn't blame her. Hell, this was a whole new world for her, one she hadn't been in as an adult. She wouldn't be pampered.

Within minutes of the marine announcing their arrival, DEA agents had swarmed them like the bugs in the jungle, surrounding Isabella, separating her from him.

"Wait, wait," Alex called, trying to get to her. She was scared, he could see it in her wide eyes, the way she sought him. Damn, they were treating her like a criminal, patting her down, cuffing her and dumping out her pack.

One of the agents took the pink vibrator and twisted it open violently. Alex recognized the device that she'd slipped in the battery pack—a portable thumb drive.

"This is everything Eric told me to look for on Santiago's computer," she said softly.

Alex couldn't explain why her words kicked him in the chest. She hadn't told him she had that information. Okay, just because she had the drive didn't mean she knew what was on it, but she didn't trust him enough to tell him she was carrying something so important.

Hell, what did it matter? He'd done his best to get her back here as quickly as possible. He wouldn't have done anything differently. But now he was going to have to answer for not knowing.

Still, as the agents pulled her in one direction and him in another for debriefing, he called, "She needs medical attention. For her feet."

Isabella held his eyes as long as she could—he wasn't sure what she was trying to tell him—before she disappeared into the building, surrounded by men in suits.

After his own debriefing, Alex walked out of the embassy to the nearby hotel recommended by the staff. He forced himself to stop wondering how Isabella was holding up. She'd probably charmed the entire intelligence agency before they released her and sent her over to the hotel.

One of the marines delivered his mail packet as he exited the conference room, and Alex returned the crisp salute with a halfhearted one of his own before he pawed through the tied-together packet. Four letters from his dad—his foster father—and two from Rebecca. He grinned. In anticipation, he stopped for a six pack, then went to his room and dug in, saving the letters from Rebecca for last.

Now the words blurred in front of him, only partially because of the tequila he'd bought when the store didn't have any brands of beer he'd heard of. Turned out, he was glad of it. Beer couldn't get him drunk enough, and he needed to get drunk.

He'd guessed what was coming from one of his dad's letters.

Keep your head.

Life doesn't always go as planned.

We love you no matter what.

His dad was an old soldier who wrote newsy letters, not sentimental ones, though Alex could always feel the love underneath the words.

Rebecca must have gone to his folks. That would be something she'd do, a decision she'd agonize over. Not the decision of leaving him, maybe, but the decision of telling him in a letter instead of waiting till he got home.

Better he learns before he gets home and finds you married to someone else, he could imagine his dad saying, and he tossed back another shot.

Better he find out when he's too far away to do something

foolish, like use his training to kill the guy.

He threw the shot glass across the room as hard as he could. It bounced off the wall and onto the carpet without the satisfying shatter.

Dropping to the edge of the bed, he dragged his hands over his head. She'd been too good for him. He'd known that, had hoped she wouldn't realize it, that he'd be able to make himself worthy of her by the time they married. He didn't deserve her. He prayed the man she was marrying did.

There was someone he did deserve, the woman who'd been occupying his mind and other parts for days. A woman who was in the hotel room just down the hall.

Chapter Five

Isabella jolted at the pounding on the door. Her nerves were already stretched tight from the endless grilling of the agents wanting to know what she knew about the death of Eric Reyes—or Cortez, as Alex and the soldiers called him. She couldn't tell them, couldn't relive that horror, not even for the good of the country, for the relief of his family. That she'd witnessed it was enough punishment.

They'd finally let her go, had escorted her here to the hotel outside the embassy, and she'd had a shower with actual soap for the first time in—had it only been three days since she'd left Santiago's? Still, she felt more human, more hopeful, after cleaning up. But now they were back for her.

She looked through the peephole, saw the top of a bent head.

She jumped, choking back a scream when he pounded again.

"Open up, Goddess."

Shepard.

Still shaking, she unlatched the door and turned the knob. Shepard swayed in the doorway, clearly drunk, but when he lifted his eyes to hers, she recognized his vulnerability in his sad eyes, downturned mouth.

"Shepard, what is it?"

But he didn't speak, just stepped inside the room, closing the door behind him. He slid a hand under her hair, bending to kiss her in the same movement.

She'd longed to know how he would taste, but tequila had had no part in her imagination. Not like this. When she pushed at his shoulders, he eased back to look at her, his eyes heavy lidded and filled with pain.

Then he whispered, "Isabella. I need you."

She didn't want his words to mean anything. She'd heard them before from men who didn't even know her name. She had dreamed of Shepard being different, that he might actually love her, would take care of her the way he loved and cared for Rebecca. But she was scared to hope.

Still, hope had her curling her fingers around his neck, pulling his mouth to hers.

His mouth was hard, like the rest of him, hot, commanding. His stubble rasped her tender lips as he closed his hands around her waist, his calluses snagging the silky fabric of her robe.

Then he pulled it apart.

She grasped his wrists. "Rebecca." She wouldn't betray another woman.

He frowned. "It's over."

The hope flared brighter and she was ashamed of herself for a moment. Shepard was hurting, Rebecca too, and she was taking advantage of it. He wouldn't like her any better in the morning than he had twelve hours ago but she didn't care. If it was all she could have, she was fine with that. She wanted to know what it was to be with someone who made her feel safe.

His tongue in her mouth was skilled, daring, moving in

strokes and sweeps that had her toes curling into the plush carpet. When he parted the robe a little more, the roughness of his clothes rasped her skin.

She wanted more.

He backed her up until her hips bumped the edge of the dresser, and she reached to balance herself. His fingers tangled her hair and he tugged her head back, releasing her mouth and following the line of her throat with his lips.

She moaned and felt him smile against her skin.

Then he went lower, tracing that bared strip of skin between her breasts, pausing only long enough to release the robe's tie, then down her belly.

His hot breath sent shivers over her skin. He parted her legs and his mouth was on her with the same manner of command as he'd kissed her, his lips drawing, his tongue darting, stroking her swollen flesh with amazing accuracy.

The orgasm hit her hard. She came with a keening cry, arching backwards, gripping the dresser, but he didn't stop, draining every bit of pleasure from her, adding his fingers, alternately stroking and penetrating her until she came harder, the room spinning, the only solid thing holding her up was Shepard.

As casually as if he hadn't destroyed her, he stood, watching as she sprawled helplessly in front of him, boneless. He kissed her again, his mouth wet with her, peeling her robe away, sharpening her desire. She clutched at him, sliding her hands up under his T-shirt to feel the ridges of muscle, to urge him to undress.

He stripped off his shirt and she reached for him, wanting to touch, feel, claim, but he moved back, shucking off his pants too. The erection she'd seen at the waterfall was just as magnificent, but he'd sheathed himself before she could touch him.

"Turn around," he said, and she did, on shaky legs.

He pressed a hand between her shoulder blades, bending her over the dresser so she was face to face with her own reflection in the mirror. Then he parted her legs and entered her with a powerful thrust.

Humiliation warred with arousal as she watched his face in the mirror, watched him moving, feeling the corresponding strokes. It was sexy as hell, but their first time should be face to face, looking into each other's eyes. Romantic, not sexual acrobatics.

She'd exercised her body, trained her muscles to make a man come quickly, but now she pushed the numbness aside, opened herself to the sensations and the emotions. Instead of fake words of praise for her lover, she centered on her own pleasure, wanted to draw the sensation out, to feel the pleasure he could give her.

Bracing her weight on her palms instead of her elbows, she rose up, making him work just a little harder to stay inside her. Making him need to stay inside her. She hadn't turned to her old tricks. Instead of letting her mind shut off, she reveled in the feelings he worked to give her.

"Christ, Isabella," he grunted, making shallow thrusts to find his way back to the same depth, sending tingles of pleasure through her.

Keeping him at the same angle, she backed against him, frustrating him, pleasing herself.

She took one of his hands, guided it to cover her, guided one finger down to stroke her, and she came. Hard. Out of control.

He unhooked her arm from around his neck and bent her over the dresser again, pounding into her, drawing out her pleasure till he came too, collapsing breathless and sweaty across her back.

She shouldn't have been surprised or hurt when he didn't cuddle her. Instead, he withdrew almost immediately to deal with the condom, then closed his hand around hers, almost a tender gesture.

"Let's go shower."

As she followed him to the bathroom, she got a good look at his streamlined body, no fat anywhere. She watched him lean in to adjust the water temperature, then he stepped in first and reached for her.

"I want to touch you everywhere," he said, backing under the spray to shield her.

"I think you did," she murmured shyly, not sure whether to face him after he'd seen what he could do to her, how he could make her lose control.

Gently, he turned her so her back was to him and bent his head to the curve of her shoulder, sucking the spray of water from her skin. He slid his palms down her arms, up into her hair. "So soft," he whispered.

His erection nudged her bottom before he eased back, gliding his hands over her breasts to the vee of her thighs then up again to her breasts to flick her nipples.

"Shepard," she whispered.

"Alex," he said against her skin.

"Alex." She twisted in his arms, letting her skin slide against his and she pulled his head down.

Alex closed his mouth over hers. God, she was everything he'd dreamed about and more, soft, giving, welcoming. Responsive. Every brush of his touch over her skin had her sighing or gasping, like she was some virgin who'd never been touched. Like she lived for him to touch her. So he touched her and kissed her, bending her over his arm, taking her mouth greedily, taking, taking. And she gave.

Alex didn't want to be on his feet anymore. He wanted her under him. He shut off the water and swept her up in one of the big towels, stroking it over her smooth skin. She blushed and gave him a beautiful smile. What did that mean? Had he crossed a line here? Could he stop himself if he had?

Not yet, he couldn't. He lifted her in his arms and carried her in to the bed, kneeling over her. His arousal pulsed in his blood, his need to take. He tasted her luscious mouth, the sweet curve of her throat, the lush flesh of her breasts, her dark nipples, one at a time, rolling them with his tongue, dragging moans from her. Her legs parted around his waist, and she pressed against him. The scent of her desire was like a hand, reaching out to stroke him, to entice him. His erection leapt in response, but he reined his desire in.

He was practiced at that.

He nuzzled and licked her breasts, then peeled himself away. She whimpered in protest, a gorgeous sound, but when he returned with his foil packet, she sat up and took it.

"I haven't touched you," she said softly.

Her fingertips hovered near his erection, and it took every ounce of will not to shove himself at her. If she touched him now, he didn't think he'd have any control.

But he wanted her hands on him.

He knelt on the bed, giving her implicit permission. She closed her fingers around him, stroked up toward the tip with a gentle swirling motion, again and again till he thought his teeth would pulverize with the effort not to come.

Then she lowered her head, and her cool breath rushed across his sensitive flesh.

"No," he shouted, grasping her wrist and moving as far away as he dared.

"Why not?" Her expression was puzzled when she lifted her eyes to his.

"I won't be able to hold out."

"So don't. We have all night."

He pressed the condom in her palm. "I want to fuck you."

Her eyes sharpened and narrowed, then she ripped into the condom and sheathed him with one businesslike move before she lay back on the bed, her eyes losing the dreamy pleasure from earlier. "Fuck away."

The change in her chilled him. This was what he wanted, sex with no strings. So why did her sudden detachment make him hesitate? He saw two people in her. Which one did he want to screw? Being with the whore would be easier, less complicated, but something about the soft Bella made him want to soothe her.

He stretched out beside her, pushing her wet hair back from her face. "Don't be like that, Bella. I want you in a bed. Is there something wrong with that?"

She reached up, stroked his cheek, but her expression remained remote. "No. Nothing wrong with that." She drew him over her and into her, and he didn't think anymore.

Chapter Six

He was gone. She had expected nothing less. Last night had been something—punishment, retribution, something. But not love.

She knew better than to believe in love. A man never did more with a woman than use her for his own good. Alex hadn't told her why he'd come, had never told her what happened with Rebecca. He'd just fucked her.

God, she hated that word.

Now she sat in the chair, dressed in the only other outfit she'd packed besides her purloined hiking clothes and the silk dress he'd shredded in the jungle. The black suit was the most respectable piece of clothing she had, despite its microscopic skirt and deep neckline. Maybe the authorities would look at her differently today and send her on her way. She couldn't tell them any more. Not only was reliving Eric's death too painful, but they might hold her accountable. If they found her to blame, she'd never be able to get to her son before Santiago.

But if she convinced the DEA to let her go, she could get back to the States, find Hector and disappear. When that happened, this life would be behind her forever. Hopefully her son's memories of this time would fade, that he would only remember the nice, normal life she planned to give him back in Las Cruces. She ached to hold him again, couldn't wait to introduce him to her parents, couldn't wait to be loved again.

The knock came just as her stomach rumbled and she realized she hadn't had anything to eat since yesterday. This being on the run was going to do wonders for her diet. She walked to the door and peeked out, hoping against hope it was Alex. But no, it was a young marine from the embassy, white hat tucked under his arm. She opened the door.

"Are you packed and ready to go, ma'am?" he asked respectfully, though he was probably older than she was.

"Go where?" she asked.

"Home, ma'am. They're sending you back to the States today."

Alex sat ramrod straight in the hard metal chair as the head DEA agent, Agent Michaels, and his own superior officer, Captain Winters, circled him like vultures. He'd told them what had happened at Saldana's, on that mountain, but they wanted to hear it again. And again.

"What was the girl doing out of the compound?"

He resisted the urge to wipe his hand over his face in frustration. Instead he folded them in front of him on the scarred table. "I told you, sir. She said Eric Cortez had told her we were coming. She saw us as her only hope."

The other men exchanged a glance. Captain Winters spoke. "How did Saldana know we were coming? Why did Cortez trust the girl?"

"I have no idea, sir."

"Do you not?" the agent snapped.

Alex met the other man's gaze steadily and watched his temper heat. "No, sir."

Michaels turned away and signaled the two-way mirror. He

waited silently, allowing the tension in the room to rise. In a matter of moments, a marine rolled in a television set, plugged it in, and left. The captain pressed a button and Alex was watching himself having sex with Isabella.

Nerves roiled in his stomach. Christ. They'd bugged her room? From the angle, it looked like the camera was above the light fixture in the corner. His face heated with embarrassment, both at being caught and at being so damn rough with her. He had used her. Because he felt used. Goddamn, he needed to get out of here, needed to find her and apologize. That would be new. He didn't even know what to say, what he could say, to make up for his treatment.

Then, realizing the captain and Michaels were watching the video, watching Bella, he reached over and slapped the TV off.

Both men turned to face him as if they'd expected nothing less.

"You seem fairly familiar with the girl," Captain Winters observed dryly.

"Running for our lives through the jungle will do that. That—" He motioned to the screen. "What you saw, was the first time we had sex."

Michaels braced his hands on the table across from Alex. What a dick. "Doesn't matter to us if it was the first or hundred and first. She clearly trusts you."

Ohh. This was not going to be good.

"She's leaving today for Miami." Michaels straightened. "You need to follow her."

"What for?"

Captain Winters braced a hip on the edge of the table, good cop to the agent's bad cop. "Saldana is still going to be looking for her, whatever else he's up to. That will be the fastest way to get the information that is on the hard drive she brought us."

Ah, so they couldn't crack the encryption on the device she'd risked her life to bring them. Scary, if you thought about the crack techs they had in the DEA.

"Look at it this way." The captain folded his arms. "You'll be protecting her as well."

"What if she makes me?"

"That's up to you," Michaels said with a shrug. "You can follow her at a distance or play lover boy, no difference. But don't lose her."

Isabella drove by the imposing Miami mansion three times, working up her nerve. Driving a car after not doing so for four years was a challenge, but she hadn't wanted to raise suspicion by hiring a cab to pass back and forth. At least this way she'd get a better look at the place that was guarded like a fortress, complete with wrought-iron fence with wicked-looking tips on the top.

She'd been in the city three days, using part of the money she'd smuggled from Santiago's compound to buy two fake ids, complete with a credit history that set her up with a gorgeous hotel room. The other part she'd used to buy information about where Santiago's cousin's house was. Two false starts and here she was, driving past the house where her son was being held, waiting for her to come for him.

The security guard in the little building by the gate— seriously, not twenty feet from the front steps—stepped out to watch her fourth pass. Okay, maybe she should have timed it better, spaced it out more, but she'd never been the patient type.

So she tugged at the hem of her blouse, exposing more cleavage, pushed her skirt up her thighs, then pulled over and rolled down the window of the rented economy car. "Hi. I'm so lost! Can you help me?"

Men were so predictable. "What can I do for you?" he asked, not even ashamed of himself for staring at her breasts.

"I'm from out of town, and I'm supposed to be visiting my friend, but I'm sure she doesn't live in a place with houses so big." She widened her eyes in an attempt to look innocent. "I must have taken a wrong turn."

He leaned in the door. "Where are you trying to get?"

"She said she lived near Coral Gables. But she's a single mom. No way she can get something like this." She leaned over as she waved toward the magnificent stucco house.

"You have her address?" the guard asked her boobs.

Uh, for an imaginary friend with an imaginary address? No. She fumbled with the map she'd used to find this house, squinted at it, passed it to him with a sheepish grin. "It started with a P. I'm terrible with names." Seriously, she could have been a blonde.

He wasn't even suspicious. "Yeah, a lot of people get confused with all the Spanish-sounding street names. Let me have a look. Could it be Pomona? Poinciana? Perugia? Palmetto, maybe?"

She made her face brighten. "That last one—is it far from here?"

"No, babe. You just took a wrong turn off Ponce de Leon." He returned the map to her, smug as could be.

She tucked it away. "I know her house won't be as nice as this one." She sighed. "Now that would have been a vacation."

"Tell me about it. I can't even go in to use the restroom."

She widened her eyes. "Uncool."

"There are some perks." He leaned casually on the door. "I have connections to get into some of the hottest clubs in Miami. You think you and your friend would like to head down to The O tonight?"

She thought fast. He said he couldn't even get into the mansion to use the restroom. What good would getting to know him do her? But she had a better chance of being admitted if she knew him than if she didn't. She slid her thighs together. He noticed, his nostrils flaring, like he was trying to smell her.

"Even if she doesn't, I do. We don't have much nightlife where I come from."

He smiled, slow and nasty. "Okay. Meet me down there at eleven. Think you can find it?"

She let herself look sheepish. "I'll do my best."

"My name's Henry. Ask for me. They'll let you in." He straightened and slapped the door, signaling her on her way.

"I'm Bethany." She gave him one last smile and drove off, shaking all over.

From a compound in the middle of the jungle, isolated for four years, to being thrust into Miami crowds in a dark, loud disco was culture shock. She maneuvered through the crowd in her new heels and silk wrap dress. She kept her chin up, scanning the crowd for Henry. He'd seemed tall, in front of Santiago's cousin's mansion, but she couldn't be sure.

Plus, even in these heels, she was barely five six. Who knew so many tall people lived in Miami? Maybe tonight was Tall People night at The O.

Someone grasped her arm and she jolted, barely able to calm herself as she turned to face Henry, her hand over her heart.

"Oh, you scared me," she shouted over the pulsing music.

"You look fantastic."

She wondered that he could recognize her. He was staring at her breasts again. She'd expected it, though, and hadn't worn a bra beneath the soft fabric. She could see by the light in his eyes that he liked it.

Whatever it took to find out where her son was.

"Did your friend come?" he asked as he led her through the crowd to an alcove, guarded by another big guy. Henry nodded at the man as he passed, but the men didn't make eye contact.

Was he taking her back there to fuck her? Here? She was willing to sleep with him to get inside the mansion. Doing so would erase Alex's touch on her skin, but she could make the sacrifice if it meant getting to her son. She'd be damned if she slept with him before she got what she wanted. She was done with that.

He started up the steps to what looked like a plush and cozy booth, the stage already set with two glasses and a bottle of wine. Seriously, did the guy get laid this way?

She'd certainly led him to believe he would get lucky tonight.

Slowly he turned as she tugged at the sleeve of his expensive suit. He lifted one dark eyebrow in question.

"I love this song. Let's dance."

He opened his mouth to protest, but she was already moving away toward the floor, beckoning him to follow with a wiggle of her breasts. Reluctantly he did, and she rewarded him with a slide of her ass against his crotch.

God. He had been ready to fuck her. She needed to keep him out on the floor as long as she could.

He leaned down as the next song started. "I got us some good stuff back at the table."

"Oh, one more song, please?" She widened eyes. "I never get to go dancing back home." That wasn't a lie.

He grunted, and this time she hooked an arm around his neck and pressed against him, shimmied, then moved away.

Again he tried to lure her to the alcove, but she backed up. "I have to powder my nose." Did women still say that? She hadn't had much human interface the past four years, only what she saw on TV.

Apparently he understood her, because he pointed in the right direction. But she could sense his frustration. She would have to get him off, but leave him wanting more so he'd take her back to the mansion.

A hand clamped over her mouth as she approached the women's restroom and a hard body propelled her forward through the door. She struggled for balance, impossible in the shoes and she whipped her head up.

And met Alex's eyes in the mirror in front of her.

"Alex," she gasped when he released her, her heart swelling, only to be deflated by suspicion. She wheeled on him. "You followed me?"

His eyes were black, his brow furrowed. "Keep it down. What the hell do you think you're doing out there?"

She tossed her hair over her shoulder. "You know why I'm here."

"I know why you're here, but not *here*." He pointed to the floor to emphasize this particular place.

God, he looked wonderful, in a black tank top that clung to his muscles, baggy khaki pants. But everything about him screamed narc. "How did you get in?"

"This isn't my first time following someone," he said.

"You'd tell me but then you'd have to kill me?"

"Something like that." He eased back from her just a bit. "Quit changing the subject. Why are you seducing the security guard?"

"How did you—?"

"Like I said, not my first time. He's not there, Goddess."

A moment passed before she realized he meant Hector. "Do you know where he is?" she asked, not daring to hope.

"Not yet, but Jesus, Bella, you're playing with fire out there. God, look at you. Every man can see every detail of your body." His gaze moved over her figure. "The way you're dancing him like a pole—"

She didn't want to hear those words from him. "He could know where Hector is."

"You think Santiago keeps him in the loop?" Alex scowled. "We've got to get you out of here without your friend seeing."

Tears sprang to her eyes, blinding her. "If Hector's not there, Alex, I don't know where else to look."

Sympathy softened his expression for a split second before the door swung in. Isabella barely registered the chatter of female voices before Alex leaned in, parting her legs with his thigh, and kissed her, hot and hard.

She found her breath but not her sense and curled her fingers behind his head, holding him down to her, kissing him back hungrily, darting her tongue in for a taste of him. Scotch this time, and he wasn't drunk with it, though he was acting strangely.

Before she could think about it, his hand slid inside the front of her dress, curving over her breast, his thumb rubbing over her nipple before he released the hook, letting the dress fall open.

Then, as he started to move against her, she got it. He wanted the intruders to think he was fucking her in the restroom, to explain his presence.

Asshole.

He nipped at her lip with his teeth, to warn her, she knew, and she gave a throaty moan. His muscles quivered beneath her touch as she explored him, before gripping his ass and grinding against him.

This time he moaned, and released her mouth, her breast, to brace himself on the sink as he thrust against her, again and again, as hard as he'd been that night in Tegucigalpa.

She opened her eyes to see the door swing shut. The women had gone.

She shoved at his shoulders and he staggered back a step, his eyes dark with desire. He struggled to extinguish it as she closed her dress and she wasn't sure why his effort hurt so much.

"You can swear to me my son is not in that house, and no one in that house can help me find him?" she asked, her own voice husky, which lit another little flare of interest in Alex's eyes.

"I have it on the best knowledge he's not in there."

"Someone you trust?" He didn't trust anyone.

"I've seen enough intelligence gathered on the house to draw my own conclusions."

"Then what do we do?"

"We get out of here without Sasquatch seeing us, and we go from there."

Not much of a plan, but she hadn't had much of one when she came to Miami. She was at square one again.

"All right. Let's go."

Isabella strode over to the door, and Alex took a deep breath to clear his head. His ploy had seemed like a good idea at the time, but it hadn't been acting, on either of their parts. If he'd been able to get his zipper down, he would have been fucking her for real.

In a bathroom.

When she was only looking for her son.

Like he needed proof he was a bastard.

When she opened the door, he heard a woman on the other side saying, "Some woman is in there fucking her boyfriend," and he reached the door in time to scoop an arm around Isabella's waist, tuck her against him. He didn't want her recognized by anyone out there. He eased out into the narrow hallway, putting his body between the woman and Isabella, flashing the woman his best smile. Beside him, Isabella gasped.

The woman was talking to Sasquatch, who saw Isabella right away, narrowed his eyes and set his teeth when he saw Alex's arm around her.

Crap.

Alex pivoted Isabella in the opposite direction and stepped between her and Sasquatch. He remembered the heels she was wearing and knew she'd need time to get away in those things. He cursed himself for not noticing if there was an exit in that direction.

The man gave Alex a dismissive glare, and called after Bella. Only he didn't use her real name, called her something like Bethany. Smart girl. No connections.

Alex wanted to look over his shoulder, make sure she was heading out, but he didn't dare take his eyes from the behemoth bellowing her alias. Alex played drunk, weaving in front of Henry one way, then the other, as the man tried to pass him to get to Isabella.

"Dude." Alex laughed drunkenly, holding up his hands in apology. His eyes narrowed, not missing anything. Like the frustration on Henry's face.

Henry shoved him out of the way and bolted past him to Isabella, who, Jesus, was coming back this way, her eyes huge, and damn, he thought he could see her knees shaking in that short dress.

"I'm sorry, Henry, I have to go. My brother came to find me," she was babbling.

"Her brother?" demanded the girl Henry had been talking to. "She was screwing her brother?"

God save him from loud-mouthed women. Alex ducked past Henry, grabbed Isabella's arm, and started to run. With a roar, the security guard followed. Alex pushed Isabella ahead of him, putting his body between hers and danger, through the crowded hallway, into the club, onto the dance floor. He could feel her heart hammering.

She was going to fall. Only his hands on her waist kept her upright, only his pressure on her kept her moving forward through the crowd that didn't want to part for her, that cast her dirty looks she caught in her peripheral vision because he was pushing her, but holding her up at the same time.

She realized she was heading toward the very alcove she'd been trying to avoid earlier, and she tried to steer away, but the crowd, and Alex, wouldn't let her.

Even though she was looking straight into Santiago Saldana's light eyes.

Chapter Seven

What the hell? She'd stopped on a dime, and he couldn't make her move forward. Afraid to loosen his hold—afraid she might drift away in this crowd—he edged in front of her and tugged.

She didn't move.

"*Bella.*"

Over his shoulder, he saw Henry approaching fast, head and shoulders above the rest of the crowd.

"Santiago's here." But she wasn't looking behind her. She stared straight ahead.

"Yeah, he's almost here." Did she think he didn't see the giant gaining on them? "*Go.*"

"No, Santiago," she said, her voice almost a squeak, and she turned then, her eyes huge and round.

His heart kicked and he glanced over his shoulder. Christ. And him without a weapon, without backup. He whipped around to the direction she'd been looking, and saw nothing. An empty private booth.

"You're imagining it," he said, but had the creeping suspicion she wasn't. Still, he couldn't protect her here. "We've got to go."

Something he said reached her and he propelled her

forward, though she kept looking over her shoulder at that alcove. Knowing he was probably bruising the soft skin of her arm, he shoved her toward the door, not looking to see if Henry was on their tail. He maneuvered them across the lot toward his truck, unlocking it with the remote and swinging her up even as he opened the door, then shoved her over and climbed in after her. He jammed the key in the ignition and gunned the engine before he looked up to see Henry charging from the front door, followed by two others, all with guns.

He swore, then shouted, "Get down," as he shifted into gear and peeled away from the curb, into the street, swerving to avoid hitting an oncoming car before punching the accelerator.

He made two turns before he looked at Isabella, still crouched on the floor. "You can get up now."

When she did, he could damn near feel her shaking across the cab.

"Are you okay?" he asked.

She nodded, but her hands trembled as she buckled herself in.

"Does Henry know where you're staying?"

She shook her head, pushed her hair back from her face. "I told him I was staying with a friend."

He turned toward her hotel and she slid him a surprised look.

"How long were you following me?" she asked suspiciously.

"I picked up your trail before you rented your Nissan." A thought occurred to him and he scowled. "If this guy wants to find you bad enough, he could."

"So I suppose it's a good thing I registered in a different hotel with my credit card and paid cash for the one I'm staying in."

He grinned despite himself. But instead of praising her, he said, "Nice place?"

She grinned back. "Oh, yeah."

Alex whistled low when he entered the luxurious room with the magnificent view of Miami. He headed for the window and opened the door to the balcony, then stepped outside. Isabella latched the door, knowing it wouldn't do much good against Santiago if he found out where she was and really wanted to come after her.

But Alex was here now, and just knowing that made her feel safer than it should. The idea that he'd followed her to Miami after the way he'd left her in the Honduras hotel room buoyed her spirits. He'd gotten her out of the jungle. He would help her find her son.

She buried the romantic notions that wanted to accompany the realization he'd come for her. Giving into those had gotten her into trouble in the past. Alex was bound to have an ulterior motive.

She loosened the tie of her dress and turned into the marble tiled bathroom. "I'm going to shower," she called to Alex and closed the door before he could answer.

She didn't lock it. He could come in if he wanted to. As battered as she was feeling, she would welcome him. He'd saved her from Santiago, though she wasn't sure he believed that.

She turned the gold fixtures till steaming water poured out, ducked under to wash the sweat and nerves away, the fear and the arousal.

When she stepped out of the bathroom, wrapped in the plush robe the hotel provided, Alex was stretched out on her king-sized bed, propped against the headboard, watching baseball with his bare feet on the mattress, holding a beer from the minifridge.

"My hero," she murmured, and he smirked.

So what had all that bluster in the jungle been about? Did the situation then have him scared, stressed, what? Or did he just think he was going to get some tonight?

Her body wouldn't mind. Her blood hummed even ten feet away from him. Alone in a room, all the privacy they could ask for. But her brain wouldn't settle down.

"Alex." She sat on the edge of the bed, making sure she left a safe distance between them. "If Hector isn't with Santiago's cousin, where could he be? Where do we look next?"

Alex muted the TV and sat up, serious now.

"What made you think Hector was there?" he asked.

"Santiago said he sent him to his cousin's."

"You believed him."

She drew back. "He was taking my son from me, sending him to a place I had no dream of being able to get to. Why wouldn't I believe him?"

Some of the tension drained from him. "How did you find the address?"

"I paid for the information. I was so sure." Despair pushed her voice out in a wail.

"Okay, okay, calm down." He held out his hands. "I can look into it, see what kind of connections he has in the States. You gave the DEA a list of names, the people who'd left the compound. We can follow any leads from that."

Everything collapsed inside her. "How long will that take?" She could barely force the words out.

"I can't promise it will be overnight, but we won't stop till we find him."

She looked at him with tears in her eyes. "Why would you do this for me? This isn't your job."

She watched him draw back into himself. There was more to this than he was letting on. She'd been right to hold back those rescue fantasies.

"Why did you show up at the club? Why are you following me?"

"We need Saldana."

She'd thought she couldn't drop farther. He was here because of Santiago. She'd been so glad to see him, so glad to touch him, to lean on him, and he was here to use her.

Well, she'd use him as well. He would find her son for her.

"Make the calls," she said. "I'll do whatever it takes to get my son back." She knew the price he'd ask. It wouldn't be a hardship.

"I'll call. But first." He leaned over her, bracing his arms on either side of her hips. "I'm going to use your shower." He straightened and headed for the bathroom.

Her heart took a long time to stop pounding.

Alex felt more human as he walked out of the bathroom in his skivvies. He'd taken care of the arousal that plagued him every moment he was with her.

There she was, curled up in bed reading a romance novel with a castle and a knight on the cover, for God's sake, and she had kittens on her pajamas. Kittens and rainbows.

Pajamas.

Kittens.

Rainbows.

What the hell? Where was the seductress? He needed the

seductress, needed the shield. He didn't know what to do with this innocent girl.

She looked up, blinked to focus.

"How old are you?" he asked suddenly. She was a mother, but that didn't mean much.

"Twenty-four."

He relaxed a little, then looked at the bed. She tucked a bookmark into her book, turned toward him and reached for the buttons of her kitten pajamas, her eyes focused on his face.

"What are you doing?" he choked.

"I told you I'd do anything to bring my son home."

He took a step back. "I won't screw you in payment for getting to your son. I'm not that big of an asshole."

She frowned and her hand stilled. "But, the bed."

"It's a big bed." He hoped. "I'm not going to attack you in your sleep."

"I know." But she seemed to hold her breath while he walked around to the other side, tugged back the covers and climbed in. When he glanced over, she seemed to have drawn into herself, gotten smaller.

"Are you scared of me?"

"No."

She almost sounded sure.

"I know you won't make me do anything I don't want to do." She gave a soft laugh. "But I know you can make me want to do things."

He turned toward her on his side. She wanted him. The knowledge was enough to give him a big...ego. "Really?"

She looked over her shoulder at him, but he could feel her nearly vibrate with nerves. "Just like that."

"Just like that." He chuckled. "You going to turn the light out soon?"

"Is it keeping you up?"

No, that wasn't what was keeping him up. The curve of her body beneath the covers, the warmth of her, the scent of her, that did it. "I can sleep through anything," he said.

"Okay. If you don't mind, I'll read a little more."

He closed his eyes. It was damned domestic, is what it was. Nice. His eyes popped open at the thought.

"Alex? Are you asleep?"

He hadn't thought he was, but the room was dark now, and he didn't remember Isabella turning off the lights.

"Yeah." He was pretty sure his croaky voice gave him away. "What? Bad dream?"

"I haven't been to sleep yet."

"What do you need, Goddess?"

"Do you have kids?"

Her voice in the dark was soft, young, none of the husky tone or crisp banter he was accustomed to hearing. He rolled onto his back.

"No. No kids."

"Do you wish you did?"

"I'm not home much. Wouldn't be any good for them."

"Boys need their daddies," she said, but her tone was more wistful than truthful.

He wouldn't know. There'd been no father figure in his life till almost too late. She hadn't been looking for a response from him.

"I love being a mom." Warmth infused her voice, reached across the bed to him, like she'd moved closer. "I never had brothers or sisters, so I wasn't around babies much. I learned everything with Hector. I mean, I wasn't totally on my own. One of Santiago's housekeepers had something like six kids, and she helped me, but everything I learned about taking care of him made me stronger."

Goddamn, he wanted to reach across the bed, to the girl who'd been alone in the compound, away from her family. Where had her family been? Had she wanted them, or had she run away from them? Maybe her parents hadn't been any better than his own.

"He was talking before he was two, in two languages, and he already knew his alphabet."

"You were with him all the time." Probably the only person she had to talk to, the only person she could trust. What had she called him? Her pure?

"Except when Santiago needed me." Her voice took on a hard edge.

"But Santiago didn't spend much time with him." Not exactly the father figure she'd been talking about.

"Hector was afraid of him. It was mostly my fault. I'd get upset when Santiago would send someone to take Hector away. Hector would sense that and cry."

He'd take the child away so Isabella could whore for him. But the idea, while it still twisted his gut, didn't disgust him the way it had. Yeah, she'd made some bad decisions, but she'd tried to make the best of it. She'd tried to make a home for her son. Better than his own mom had done. *She* couldn't get rid of him fast enough to get to her whoring. Sometimes she hadn't even bothered.

He tightened his grip on the pillow to keep from reaching

for Isabella. She still wasn't right for him. He wasn't right for her. But it felt better knowing what she was about.

"Do you think Saldana could be making up for lost time with Hector? Sometimes, once kids reach a certain age, men finally want something to do with them."

Her soft gasp in the dark told him she'd taken his words wrong.

"Not that. Men just—babies scare them." Damn, he was trying to make her feel better, and he was rusty. "Not—I didn't mean—" Though he knew it was reality in too many cases. Saldana was a depraved son of a bitch. "I meant in a fatherly way."

She snuffled a laugh. "No. Santiago only wanted Hector to prove he had a son. He won't be having more. He just—having a son made him feel like a man."

"Like hurting you did."

"I'm a grown-up. I made the choice. Hector didn't." She sounded so lost. His hand slid marginally closer to her.

"How did you end up there?"

She shifted, and he could almost feel her breath on his skin. "I'm not like you, Alex. It was scary for me to be in a strange place. Santiago made me feel safe. At least for a while."

"Yeah, you said, but how? I mean, you probably had a lot of admirers. Why him?"

"Because I'm shallow. He was wealthy and charming, and that appealed to me."

Alex was strong and brave, just what she needed now. Good to remind him.

He pulled back. "We better get some sleep."

He heard the soft intake of breath that told him he'd surprised her, but he deliberately closed his eyes and shut her out.

"Alex?"

"Go to sleep."

"Did you make that call to the DEA?"

He swore and swung out of bed, reaching for his phone. He walked out into the hall to make the call, and when he slipped back into bed, she whispered, "Thank you."

Alex got up, trying not to disturb the mattress and the woman sleeping on it. Isabella had managed to stay on her side of the bed and he still had a raging hard-on, just from smelling her, hearing her soft breathing.

Being around her was going to be great for his self-control.

"I can take care of that for you."

He froze at the end of the bed. "What?"

She sat up, pushing her dark tumbled hair back from her face. In the dim light through the crack in the curtains, she looked like a wet dream, even in the kitten pajamas.

She was looking at his tented boxers.

"Christ." He shifted his weight to hide his erection.

"Come here." She gave him her seductress smile.

"No."

"Are you afraid of me?" She tossed back his question from last night. "I'm very good at it. It might get rid of some of the tension between us."

Were they talking about the same thing? "You think us having sex again is going to get rid of the tension? It's only going to add to it."

She smiled slowly. "I was talking about a blow job and yes, if you let go of your ideas about sex, it will release the tension."

He turned to face her, leaning one shoulder on the wall. "So it really doesn't mean anything more than that? A physical release?" She was trying too hard to convince him.

She drew her legs up and wrapped her arms around her knees, cocking her head and smiling. "I can't afford for it to be anything else."

"That's sad as hell," he said, and pushed away from the wall to go into the bathroom. Christ, what a sad life she'd had if that was her perspective. Sure, he was no virgin, and he'd hooked up out of desire more than love most times, but there had to be something more to sex than just getting off.

He was in the shower when the door opened. He shoved open the shower curtain and glared. "Damn it, Goddess, I told you—"

She held out his cell. "You have a call. I thought it might be about Hector."

She'd answered the phone. Christ. He was going to catch hell.

He took the phone from her and closed his eyes to avoid her hopeful gaze.

"You're in her hotel room?" was the first question from Captain Winters, his tone disbelieving. "In her shower?"

Alex couldn't think of anything to say.

"You were supposed to follow her, not move in."

"She got into some trouble last night. I stepped in."

"You're there to find Saldana, not to protect her."

"If she gets hurt, she's not going to do us any good," he said, choking back his frustration. Hadn't the captain put him in this position, told him to do whatever was necessary?

"You don't know if you can trust her to lead you to Saldana."

He looked at Isabella, who watched him, lips pressed together anxiously. "You think she's working with him?" He had a suspicious mind, but even he could see she never would do that. Of course, he knew her better than the captain.

He motioned for her to leave but she folded her arms under her breasts and shook her head. He widened his eyes at her to assert his point and gestured toward the door. She unfolded her hands and moved toward him. Jumping back, he tugged the shower curtain across his hips and scowled. With a chiding look, she reached around to shut off the water. Then she leaned one hip against the sink and waited for him to resume his conversation.

"We're looking for the kid," he told his captain. "We think Saldana might be where the kid is."

"What kid?"

"What kid?" he repeated. "Her kid. Saldana's kid. He took him away from her to punish her."

"We don't have any information on a kid."

Chills rose up over his skin that had nothing to do with being wet in the draft from the open door. Had she lied to him? He didn't want to believe she would lie about something like that, so he pressed.

"His name is Hector. He's three years old. Born at the compound." He looked to Isabella for confirmation. "He was born..." He waited for Isabella to supply the info.

"September 12, 2007," she said.

He repeated it into the phone.

"We don't have any intel on a kid," Captain Winters repeated.

Alex scrambled for an explanation. "So Saldana hid the info, didn't let him go near windows or anything so you couldn't get pictures."

"Except he had to order his supplies from the outside world. There were no diaper deliveries, bottles, none of the stuff you need for a baby. There was no baby."

Alex's stomach heaved and he barely registered the info he was given as he looked at Isabella's stricken face.

"Yeah, okay," he said to acknowledge the list of names and places Saldana might be.

"We've got people on these men already. We need you to stick with the girl, get her to trust you."

Trust. What did she know about trust? But the minute he flipped the phone closed, he took two steps toward Isabella. He yanked the waistband of her pajamas down and pushed her shirt up.

"What—?" She shoved at his hands and he lowered his head. "What are you doing?"

"Looking for stretch marks." And not finding any. He traced his fingertips across her smooth—very smooth—skin. Watched it jump under his touch. Backed away and glared. "You didn't have a baby."

"What?" She tugged her clothes back in place, her movements shaky as she stared at him as though he'd lost his mind.

"You never had a baby." He snatched up a towel and whipped open the door.

Isabella stood frozen for a moment. What had they said to him to make him think she was lying? Not that it took much for him to think badly about her. She dragged her hair back from her face, pushed away from the sink and followed him.

He was pulling on jeans even though droplets of water still glistened on his back and chest. She strode past him to her suitcase, popped it open and pawed through it, her eyes blurry.

"What are you looking for?"

She tucked her hair behind her ears and battled the tears. "Do you think I would come all this way and not have proof he's my son?" She found the bag she was looking for, turned with it in her fist.

A bag of camera film, undeveloped.

He looked at them. "What's this?"

"Pictures of me and Hector."

"Pictures." He paused in the middle of pulling on his shirt, with the T-shirt caught at his elbows. "Not even developed. You don't have like a birth certificate or something?"

"I looked." Her voice rose in desperation. "I couldn't find it. Santiago must have hidden it so I would never claim my boy."

He pulled his shirt on the rest of the way. "My people said there were never any diapers delivered, no baby food, none of the stuff babies need."

His words staggered her and she pressed her palm to her middle in shock. "You know what was delivered to our house?"

"Sweetheart, I know what kind of tampons you used."

Embarrassment threatened to swamp her. She fought back against it and lifted her chin. "Then you know that for nine months I didn't get any tampons."

He blinked at that. "I'll check into it. Do you have any other proof?"

She set the packet of film down and went back through her bag. Santiago had sent most of Hector's things away with him, hadn't allowed her to keep any of Hector's belongings in her room in case his clients saw them—mothers weren't sexy—but she'd smuggled some keepsakes, kept them buried beneath her silks. She found the locket, squeezed her fingers over it before turning to hold it out to Alex.

"A lock of hair from his first haircut."

Alex took the locket, opened it, touched the fine dark hair inside with his fingertip. She could sense something softening in him.

"You could get a DNA sample from it, couldn't you?"

He looked up, considering. "Maybe."

"I don't have stretch marks because Santiago insisted I take care of myself. His housekeeper, Senora Gamez, made a cream for me, and she helped me apply it twice a day. Santiago wouldn't pay for diapers, and we'd have too much trouble disposing them anyway, so we used cloth diapers. I had a wet nurse, a girl from nearby. Santiago didn't want any more wear and tear on my body than need be, and besides, a lactating woman is not sexy." She couldn't hide the bitterness in her voice. Her hand hovered near the locket. "So, do you need the hair for DNA?"

He snicked the locket shut. "No, we don't need to do that."

The tension that had been humming through her since the phone rang eased a bit. "You believe me?" she asked, not wanting to hope.

"Yeah." He held the locket by its chain. "Yeah." He stepped back, not looking at her. "Look, stay here. I've got a meeting to get to."

"I'll go with you." The last thing she wanted was to be prisoner again, no matter how luxurious the room.

He shook his head and dropped to the edge of the bed to put on his boots. "You draw too much attention. You need to lay low."

"I thought you wanted me to draw him out."

"We don't even know if he's here. You'll be safer waiting for me."

"I can't. I need to find my son. Every day he's away from me is another day he'll have the chance to forget me."

"I don't have any leads on the kid." He sounded like he regretted it.

"So what do we do?"

"We wait. We think. We reason it out. But I want you to stay here." He picked up his jacket and strode toward the door.

"Shepard." Captain Winters greeted Alex at the doorway of the DEA office.

The man was in full uniform, and Alex only had a shirt to throw over his tank top and cargo pants from the previous night. He hated being out of uniform when the situation called for it, and it seemed the situation called for it.

But the captain didn't say anything about his state of dress, only turned smartly on his heel and started down the hall. Alex stayed in step.

"You connected with the girl last night."

"Yes, sir. I found her at a nightclub. She's determined to find someone who knows where her child is."

Captain Winters made a sound in his throat.

"Sir?"

"We were able to decode some of the files she smuggled out."

Alex was unprepared for the slap of emotion that accompanied the news. Would he be free of Isabella then? Did he want to be?

Hell, yes, he did, before he made a damn fool of himself again. "Anything useful?"

"We know what happened with the girl and Agent Cortez."

A ball of ice dropped into his belly. "Sir?" he managed.

The captain looked at him with something like sympathy. "Come see for yourself."

He led Alex into a darkened room with a large computer monitor on the desk. The captain introduced Alex to the agent in charge, Agent O'Malley, and the two techs at the table. Alex nodded greetings to them but his attention was already on the screen. What would he see, and why was it important that he see it?

"The first file we were able to open is Cortez."

At the captain's nod, the tech started the video. Alex took a step closer.

"Why was this encoded?" Alex asked, hiding a wince as Cortez's battered face appeared on the plasma screen.

"Because it's proof they had a US agent," O'Malley said.

Alex distanced himself from the man being tortured on the screen. He let himself think of it as a TV program as the man silently suffered random blows to the face from a guy with fists the size of a Mack truck.

A door opened on screen, and Isabella stumbled in. After a moment, Alex could see someone had his fist wrapped in her hair, holding her head at a painful angle. She made a choked sound when she saw Cortez, and he went stiff at the sight of her. Too late, he'd given himself away. The agent was in love with her.

"What is he to you?" the man holding her demanded.

"Nothing," she gasped.

"Liar! What is he to you?" the man screamed.

She flinched from the sound and cried out when he twisted her hair. Cortez said her name, very softly, and Isabella opened

110

her eyes to look at him, her expression sorrowful.

The ham-fisted man moved in front of Cortez, but not blocking his face from the camera. He lifted a knife to Cortez's cheek.

"Do you want this to be the last thing you see?" the man—Saldana? Alex couldn't tell, his face was obscured—asked, leaning close to Cortez, dragging Isabella with him.

Cortez's gaze flicked to Isabella's. She was sobbing.

Mack Truck dug the knife in.

"Do not close your eyes," Saldana growled to Isabella, "or you will be next."

So she didn't. She watched. Because she didn't look away as they carved out Cortez's eyes, neither did Alex. Winters let the video play out until Isabella's keening died away and Cortez slumped in his chair.

"The next video," Winters said crisply, as if they hadn't just watched a man die, "is her punishment."

"Why would they—? Jesus."

Saldana shoved Isabella into the room on the screen, and Alex's heart lurched before he reminded himself this was months ago, that she was safe in a Miami hotel room now. Mack Truck followed. Saldana stepped aside and Mack Truck spun Isabella toward him, tore her dress from her body with hands still stained with Cortez's blood.

She didn't fight as the man pushed her to the bed and lowered his big body over her. Of all things to help him distance himself from what he was watching, that helped the most. The woman he knew would fight. This broken woman was not her.

"Turn it off," Alex said softly, lowering his head.

Winters gave him an unreadable look, then nodded to the tech, and the room was silent.

"The kid appears later in the video. She was telling the truth. But the boy's probably dead now. Saldana probably told her he sent the kid back and just dumped his body in the jungle somewhere."

"It's his kid." Even as he said it, Alex knew it didn't mean anything. He of all people knew parentage didn't make someone human.

"You need to prepare her."

Alex shook his head. "I can't do it. It's all she's got to hold on to now."

"Shepard. You're too involved."

Panic hit him hard in the gut. He'd never been accused of that before. "Don't pull me."

"I'm not. Just watch yourself. Be aware you may never find the kid."

"Do you have any leads at all? Where Saldana might be?"

Agent O'Malley led the way out of the media room. Not that it mattered. Isabella's screams still echoed in his ears.

"A team went back to the compound, but it was burned to the ground," O'Malley said. "They salvaged what they could, but we haven't been able to get any information. Now the list of people Isabella gave us in Honduras was more helpful. We were able to track two of the people on that list into the US. We might have been able to track more if she'd known their full names."

"I don't think they were people she really wanted to know," Alex said, wondering how many times Mack Truck had been her punishment.

And wondering if she'd been thinking about that when he'd come to her room in Honduras. Christ.

"So where are these people? Here?"

"One, the woman, Carmen Ferdin, came through Florida. I don't know if she's still here. We're looking. But we're more interested in the man, Pablo Massiatte. We tracked him to Texas."

"Why are you more interested in him?"

O'Malley hooked a thumb back at the media room. "That was the guy who cut out Cortez's eyes."

Alex swore. "Isabella swore she saw Santiago at The O last night."

"So you said. We got the surveillance tapes. We weren't able to see him."

"It was crowded as hell."

"We saw the two of you."

"Nothing around us? What about in those little corners? The private tables?"

"The O has cameras at all the entrances. We didn't see him. She must have been imagining it."

"Maybe." She'd been scared and thinking about running into him. She could have imagined it. "What about me? What can I do to help find Saldana and the kid?"

"Nothing yet," Winters said, slapping him on the back. "Keep a close rein on her. We're still not sure she's trustworthy."

After what Alex had just seen, he was certain she was. If the army wouldn't help him help her, he'd find someone else who would.

Retired Sergeant Major Lionel Danes was a big man, broad, tall and heavy. He rose from the tiny table at the coffee house. His added weight didn't decrease his threatening presence, though, because all the tables surrounding him were empty.

113

Lionel embraced Alex enthusiastically, swallowing him in those beefy arms. Hell, for all the weight the guy had put on since the last Ranger reunion Alex had attended with his father, Danes wasn't soft. He hammered Alex on the back a couple of times with the flat of his palm before releasing him to sit down again and offer Alex a seat.

"How's your old man? Haven't heard from him in a while."

"Yeah, he didn't make the reunion this year. Doctors are worried about his heart. The diabetes doesn't help."

Lionel's high forehead creased in concern. "We're getting old."

Alex smiled. "No, sir, Sergeant Major."

"Why don't you go get yourself a cup of coffee and come back here and tell me what you need from me."

"Yes, sir, Sergeant Major."

Alex returned to the table with his coffee in the tall paper cup and worked through how to broach the subject. He figured the old man was like himself and would appreciate the direct approach.

"Coin check," Danes said abruptly. Alex set down his coffee on the tiny table and dug his Ranger coin out of his hip pocket, slapped it down on the table in time with the old man.

The old guy grinned and tucked his back in his breast pocket. "Good man, Shepard."

Alex sat across from him. "I need to find a bad guy."

The sergeant major snorted. "Why would you want to do that?"

"He's a really bad guy."

"What makes you think I can help you?"

"You know this city. You have connections."

"You think I have those kinds of connections?"

"Sir, with all due respect, I know you do. You were a detective in this city for twenty years."

"Yeah, but son, it's not like the Old West. There aren't just a handful of bad guys. More come in and more leave every day."

"How would I find out who's coming and who's leaving?"

The old man tilted his head, as if seeing for the first time that Alex was serious. "Who are you looking for?"

"Santiago Saldana."

Danes blew a breath out through his nose. "When you say bad, you mean bad."

"He's pretty much scum of the earth."

"Why are you looking for him?"

"He killed a DEA agent."

"Son, when did you become DEA?" Danes asked, sitting back in the frail chair, making it creak.

"I'm not. I was on the mission in Honduras, he slipped through our fingers. We think he might have a kid with him."

Danes raised his eyebrows. "Why the hell would Saldana have a kid? He's no Santa Claus."

"It's his kid."

Danes's eyes sharpened. "What do you care about his kid?"

"The kid's mom wants him back. I'm thinking we find the kid, we find Saldana. But I don't know where to look."

"That's where you need my help."

"Yes, sir."

Danes leaned forward again. "Well, let me see what I can do. How can I get hold of you?"

Frustrated that Danes didn't tell him what he could do right now, Alex scrawled his cell number on a napkin and passed it to the old man. "Whatever you can do, I'd appreciate," he made himself say before he shoved back his chair and strode out.

He hadn't even touched his coffee.

Alex returned to the hotel frustrated and empty handed. He knew it wouldn't be easy to find Saldana in the city when they hadn't been able to corner him in his own place in the jungle. Still he wasn't accustomed to trying and failing.

He got up to the room before he remembered he didn't have a key card. He knocked, but no answer. What was she doing in there? Sleeping? Showering? Damn, he was going to have to go get a key card. He headed back down to the lobby, slowed when he saw her stagger in through the glass doors, her face white, her body bent nearly double.

He raced toward her, grabbed her arms and crouched to look into her face. The pained expression, the parted lips, the glazed eyes, the shallow breaths. The video he'd just seen played through his head—what had she been through now? She gripped his arms and dug her nails into his arms, and he inspected the rest of her.

"Bella, are you hurt? Is it Saldana?"

She sucked in a breath and shook her head. "No. No."

"Bella." He gripped her wrists and guided her toward a chair in the lobby before he knelt before her.

"They're empty."

"What?" He'd barely heard her voice—it was all breath, indrawn breath.

"The rolls of film—they were empty. No pictures."

Only then did he realize she clutched a bag from a one-hour photo lab.

Pictures. This was about pictures. Irritation chased away a relief so sharp it was painful. He sat back on his heels. "You took the film in? That's what this is about?"

"There was nothing on any of the rolls," she said, tears streaming, her nose dripping. "No pictures."

"Christ, Bella, I thought you were hurt. It's just pictures."

Her head snapped up. "*Just* pictures? It's all I have." Her breath wheezed. "I have nothing. No first smile, no first step, no first tooth, nothing. If he's gone, if I never see him again, it will be like he never existed. I will have nothing of him."

Alex realized people were staring, but her pain reached out and wrapped around him.

"Come on, let's go upstairs," he said softly, taking the bag from her. She'd paid for them. Paid for blank photos. "Bella."

"He's gone, Alex. I'm not getting my baby back." Her voice had lost its shrillness, descended into hollow hopelessness that hurt to hear.

"You will. We will. I promise." He stroked a hand down her back to soothe her, heard the promise come out of his mouth, tried not to wince at the hope in her eyes. How the hell could he make that happen? Why did he want to ensure it did?

Chapter Eight

Isabella had calmed a bit by the time she got to the room, but when Alex went to throw the bag of worthless pictures away, she snatched them back and held them to her. He knew the x-ray machine they'd gone through at airport security in Tegucigalpa had probably wiped out the pictures, but she hadn't said anything about film, and who would have thought she'd have dozens of rolls of baby pictures? Hell, hadn't Santiago had the money to buy her a digital camera? He didn't know anyone who had a film camera anymore.

"Bella, they aren't going to become visible just because you want them to," he murmured.

"They were his pictures."

"No, they weren't. Not since they were ruined."

Her head came up at that and he cursed himself. Of course she'd be looking to place blame. He had to think of something to settle her down, fast.

"DEA was able to track two of the people you named from the compound into the country."

She looked at him sharply. "Who?"

"Pablo and Carmen." He watched her face carefully as he said Pablo's name. Nothing. No reaction. How had she just been able to shut that out? "Pablo's in Texas, they think, and

Carmen is in Florida."

"Do they know where?"

"Not yet. How close was Saldana to these people?"

"Pablo would do anything he said. I'm not sure about Carmen. I didn't really know anyone other than the housekeeper that well, and her only because she helped me with Hector."

"Where is she? Did she leave the compound?"

She shook her head, slumping again. "I left her behind."

He nodded, considering, but deciding not to tell her about the fire at the compound. "I wondered if she could have Hector. Would Carmen have him? Or Pablo?"

She did pale this time at the mention of Pablo's name. "No, I don't think so. I mean, they left after Santiago had sent Hector away."

"But they could have met with someone somewhere and gotten him."

For a second, just a second, hope flared in her eyes, then frustration took over. "But we don't know where they are either. Texas, Florida, we still don't know where."

"No, but we have people looking."

"While they're looking, I'm supposed to just sit here?" As if that was wrong, she pushed to her feet. Her legs wobbled a little.

"We don't have any other leads."

"We know Santiago was at The O last night."

He took a step back. Damn, he didn't want to take her where it was so difficult to protect her. But his assignment was to find Saldana through her, and he wouldn't accomplish that by sitting in the hotel.

Besides, he didn't think he could sit in this room all night, with just her, after seeing that video. Getting out would give him something else to think about.

As much as he hated it, The O was their only lead.

"What, you're going to just go up to him and demand to know where Hector is? Hell, as far as he knows, you died in the jungle."

She pressed her lips in a straight line. "Then he won't expect me to show up at The O."

"He won't be there. DEA went over the surveillance tapes from last night. They didn't see him."

She shook off his doubts. "He might have been in disguise. I saw his eyes."

"You wanted to see his eyes. I mean, you wanted to see him. Not to see *him*, but you're anxious for this to be over, to find your son."

"I saw him, Alex." She strode to the closet, flung it open. "I'm going back. It's the only thing I can do."

"They won't let me use my team for this." He sank to the bed and watched her flip through the outfits. "They don't believe he was there. I can't protect you in that place on my own."

She turned to him. "You can," she said, pressing her palm to his cheek. "I promise, I'll be good."

If this was being good, Alex was going straight to hell. He'd never seen a woman move like that, her head back, straight-shouldered stride that, goddamn it, had every man in the place turning to look at her. The skirt barely covered her ass and the skinny straps of the top barely contained her stunning breasts. She was trying to get Saldana's attention, he realized. He'd thought maybe she dressed that way to get cooperation—God knew he'd cooperate with a woman who appeared to be offering what she was offering.

"Amazing. You gave every guy in here a hard-on," he muttered, keeping his touch at the small of her back and his gaze alert for any encroachers. "Should be in the *Guinness Book of World Records* or something."

"I said I'd be good. Now you need to be." She edged up to the bar. "What do girls drink?"

He shrugged. "Hell, I don't know."

"On *Sex and the City* they drank Cosmopolitans," she said a little breathlessly. "But maybe those are out of style."

He rolled his eyes. "Give her a mojito," he told the bartender. "I'll take a beer."

Isabella leaned on the bar, deepening her already impressive cleavage. The bartender stared, reaching blindly for the bottles.

Alex wanted to punch him in the face.

"Hey, do you know where I could find Santiago Saldana?" she asked.

Alex choked on his beer. The bartender merely blinked.

"Do you know him?" Isabella pressed. "I know he comes in here."

"Nah, I don't know any customers. No guys, anyway." He gave her breasts a leering look.

Alex plucked their drinks off the bar, passed Isabella hers, then steered her away from the bar.

"What are you doing?" she demanded, fighting for balance on her heels.

"Saving you from your own heavy-handedness. Do you just plan to ask everyone who works here who knows Saldana?"

"What do you suggest?"

"Keep your eyes open." He guided her to a table just above the dance floor. She stumbled in the crowd, splashing a bit of the sticky drink on her wrist. She lifted her arm and licked it off. Alex heard a guy nearby groan, saw him slap his hand over his chest as if she was giving him a heart attack. Alex positioned himself between the man and Isabella, glowering. The groaner lifted his eyebrows in acknowledgement and backed off.

"Stand over there." He walked to the table with his back to the dance floor, against every instinct.

"Why?" she asked.

"So you can see everyone—and they can see you. Keep an eye out."

"And look good doing it?"

He saluted her with his beer and scanned the crowd as he drank. He could feel her tension even across the small table.

"We can go," he said when she shifted her weight and toyed with her glass.

"I'm just not used to this many people."

"Right."

She drank deeply and made a face. She set it down and slid it away. "Sweet."

"Yeah. Rebecca liked them."

She snapped her gaze to him, questioning. He looked out over the dance floor, edged closer to her, too uncomfortable with having his back to the door. She drew in on herself, as if she didn't want any part of herself touching him.

"Bella? Do you see anything?"

She pulled the glass toward her. "It's so crowded."

"You want to go?"

"And do nothing?" She shook her head, rolled back her shoulders, before lifting her head in resolve. "We'll stay."

She took a sip, then another, and he actually saw it take effect, wondered how often she drank, if she drank to get through what Saldana put her through. Except she was clearly affected after one drink.

She began to move to the music as she looked around. The gentle sway was unconscious. She added a tapping foot, a bounce. Did she want him to ask her to dance? He didn't dance. He looked out over the packed floor below them. He especially didn't do that, at least not in public. As one man stood, keeping time to the movement, his partner splayed her hands down his sides, writhing as she lowered herself, till her mouth was even with his belt buckle and he was thrusting his hips at her face.

He turned away to see another man pull his partner back against him. She looped an arm around his neck, her lips parted in pleasure and invitation. His fingers spread wide over her bare belly, his thumb between her breasts, his hips grinding into her ass as she circled it against him in time to the pulsing music.

Christ. Disgusted with himself for watching, for being aroused, he turned away and signaled the waitress. He ordered more drinks, despite a halfhearted protest from Isabella.

She drank quickly, until he caught her wrist, pushing it down to the table.

"You don't want a rum hangover."

"Calms my nerves."

"It'll make you sloppy. I need you clear-headed and clear-eyed."

"Right." She swallowed and slid the drink away.

MJ Fredrick

"You don't see anyone?"

"You asked me already."

He braced both hands on the table. "I think this is a waste of time."

"What else would we do? Please, Alex."

He saw the guy approaching, straightened automatically, squaring his shoulders. His size, his presence didn't deter the young man, who only had eyes for Isabella.

"You want to dance?"

Isabella looked pointedly at Alex, but he wasn't letting her use him as an excuse.

"Go ahead," he said, lifting his bottle of beer by the neck.

She drew back as if surprised by his attitude. Slow learner. Still, he thought she might blow the guy off on her own. Instead she tossed her head back with the least amount of confidence he'd ever seen in her and straightened.

"Sure." She tucked her arm through the stranger's and followed him onto the floor.

Everything in Alex went tight. He couldn't stand seeing her easy casualness with this man. He'd watched her dance with the security guard last night.

Today he'd seen evidence of what she'd told him about her life in the compound.

If this man laid a hand on her, he'd snap it off.

God, the woman couldn't help being sexy. He didn't like seeing her be sexy for someone else. Still, like every man here, his eyes were drawn to her.

She moved like a wet dream, sinuous, her movements so graceful, gorgeous. Her body in that dress had its own message, one the man she danced with received and responded to, moving closer, reaching for her. She danced backwards, as far

124

as the pressing crowd allowed. The man pursued, but with a smile, Isabella moved away to the beat of the music.

Her partner moved after her, acting like the pursuer in some cat-and-mouse game. Isabella kept her smile, but made her message—no—clear, at least to Alex.

Lover Boy wasn't as astute, though. Either he was drunk or determined, but he moved in, catching her hips. She leaned away, shoulders as far back as she could go.

Alex was on the dance floor before he thought about it, pushing his way through the crowd toward them. He caught Isabella's hand and tugged. She turned and her eyes widened, then she broke away from her partner. Alex pulled her flush against him, then glared over her shoulder at Lover Boy, who looked surprised at his suddenly empty arms. Drunk, maybe. Still, Alex didn't want to underestimate any man.

"Sorry, our song." He curved his fingers around her back and put his body between them, though he kept the guy in his peripheral vision. He'd seen enough bar fights to know the "wronged" man came at you from behind.

"We don't have a song." Her breath was warm against his throat, her words not loud enough for her former partner to overhear.

"We do now." He moved with her to the beat of the song he didn't recognize, but kept his attention on the retreating man.

"I don't need you to take care of me." She wound her arms around his neck and moved to the music.

She wasn't against him, not like he needed her to be, but he could feel every muscle in her move. He kept his hands on her back, not sliding them down to her ass and pulling her against him like he longed to do. "I didn't like the way he was grabbing at you."

She loosened her hold, folding both arms around the back

of his neck and looking into his eyes. "You still don't get it. Whatever they do to my body doesn't matter."

His grip tightened, his jaw clenched. "And me? What about what I do to your body?"

She shook her head, her expression drawn, and glanced away. "That doesn't matter either."

She didn't move out of his arms, but that didn't make him feel less like shit. Why had he wanted her answer to be different? He wasn't any different than those men who'd used her. He was just as rough, just as disrespectful. But at least his hunger had been for her, and not power over her. Not that he could expect her to see the difference.

He looked over her head, inspecting the crowd. He couldn't forget why they were here, not even with her in his arms. She, too, seemed to move without thinking, and he wondered what the hell was going on in her mind.

As soon as the song was over, she drifted away, out of his arms. He followed her, wanting to reach for her, but getting the feeling she'd shake him off.

Not that she seemed to notice he was there. She was focused on something else. Where the hell was she going?

Then he recognized the direction she was moving, leading to the tunnel heading toward the restrooms. This time he did grab her. "What are you doing?"

She widened her eyes at him in mock innocence. "I'm going to the ladies room."

He frowned. "You weren't going to say anything?"

She dropped her gaze to his fly. "I didn't want you to think it was an invitation."

He dropped her arm and passed a hand over his hair. "Christ, Bella."

"I saw someone here I wanted to talk to."

"In the restroom."

She nodded and slid her eyes toward the wall, where clearly she expected him to wait. He dropped against it with a *thunk*, but kept his gaze on her as she opened the restroom door. Every instinct wanted to shove her out of the way, give the room a once-over and make sure she was safe.

Who had she seen in there?

His body was on high alert, and he tightened up each time someone came down the hall.

Which was often, because of where the hall led.

Just when he'd had enough, she came out, smiling over her shoulder at someone. When she turned to Alex, she had a hint of the smile left, but it faded quickly. Why was she so pissed at him again? Something about him protecting her?

"We missed a step." She motioned him to follow her down the tunnel, away from the noise.

What the hell? But he followed, hating the disconnected feeling. When had he started feeling connected?

"What made us think Santiago would come here under his own name?" she asked, her words quick in her excitement. "Of course he wouldn't. I never even thought of that."

Alex had thought of that, as had the DEA, but he let her continue.

"I saw the waitress from last night."

As if that answered everything. "In the restroom?"

"Yeah, and I asked her about Santiago. Only he's not going by that name."

Okay. Just maybe Isabella had stumbled onto something they didn't know. He glanced back toward the bathroom.

"You ready to go then?"

She turned her gaze back toward the club and bit the inside of her lower lip. "Yeah, I guess there's nothing else we can do here," she said with a sigh.

"You have that waitress's name?"

She turned back to him with a frown. "Of course."

He nodded toward the door, dropping his hand to her waist, glad to be in control of the situation again. "Let's go, then."

They slipped out the door—dozens of people were queued up to get in—and headed for his truck. All the time he kept one eye on her and another on the crowd. Isabella made a beeline for the passenger door, but he caught her hand, pulling her against him while he scanned the area to see if anyone was behind them.

She scowled. "I wonder if you'll ever do that because you want to."

She broke away, but he'd had enough time to be satisfied they weren't followed.

That was the only thing he was satisfied about.

"What name did you get?" he asked, once they were safely on the road back to the hotel, tail free.

"Guillermo Morales. Georgia said he used a credit card with that name."

He could hear the excitement, the sense of accomplishment in her voice. "She's sure it's the same guy? Doesn't seem to me he'd be dumb enough to use a credit card, you know?"

"I thought so too, but she was very clear about his description. Late forties, heavy accent, light eyes."

Alex shook his head. "Seems that could apply to a lot of guys in this city. What was the name again?" He fished his phone out of his front pocket as he maneuvered through traffic, flipped it open and dialed with his thumb. He glanced over at her as he lifted the phone to his ear. "She was sure?"

She nodded and reached down to slide off her shoes.

"Yeah, it's Shepard," he said when Agent O'Malley answered. "We need to know if Guillermo Morales is one of Saldana's aliases."

"Where did you get that name?" O'Malley asked.

"We went back to the nightclub to see if Isabella could see him again, maybe draw him out."

"You got this name how?"

Alex told him, heard typing through the phone.

"No." Surprise laced O'Malley's voice. "We don't have that as an alias. This waitress, she seemed dependable?"

"Isabella said she was." He glanced over at Isabella, who was watching, ready to jump out of her skin. "Her name was Georgia..." He trailed off, motioning for Isabella to supply the rest of the name.

"Brady."

He repeated the name into the phone.

"We'll pick her up, run this guy's cards, see where he's been," O'Malley said, but no excitement infused his voice. He wasn't expecting much to come of this, Alex could tell. That, he wouldn't pass on to Isabella.

"You'll let us know what you find out."

"Yeah, I mean, if you check back in, we'll tell you what we found."

Alex ended the call. He couldn't ask for more than that.

They got back to the hotel room in silence. Once they walked in, Isabella kicked off her shoes and pulled off her blouse as she headed into the bathroom.

Alex stared at the curve of her breast. "I wish you wouldn't do that."

She looked over her shoulder at him. "I'm hot. I'm going to shower."

"Then wait till you're in the bathroom to get undressed," he snapped.

She turned to face him fully. Her scent, damp, sexy, forbidden, washed over him. He forced himself to look into her eyes.

"Why does it bother you?" she demanded, then stepped closer, sliding her fingers over the fly of his pants. "Does it make you want me?"

He choked as his erection jumped against her touch. He took a step toward her, hoping to intimidate as he leaned against her, pressing her to the wall, propping his arm over her head. Her gaze didn't falter—he was small potatoes compared to what she'd endured.

"I always want you."

She took a deep breath so that her breasts lifted and brushed against his chest. Her fingers closed around his erection through his pants and he ground his teeth to stop himself from grabbing her hips, pushing up that skirt—

"Then have me," she said in that throaty voice, her eyes dark, unreadable.

All the blood rushed from his head. "It can't happen."

Her eyes flashed, just a moment, before icing over. "Because I'm a whore."

That wasn't it. He didn't really want her thinking that was the reason, but he seized onto it anyway. He pushed away from the wall, hating the loss of her touch, the look in her eyes. But he didn't think she'd buy the idea that he believed she deserved more, that she deserved a man who could love her, could treat her right. Not a man who wasn't above using her.

She needed to know what love, what lovemaking, was. He wasn't the man to show her.

"Why do you stay here with me, then? Get another room."

She was pissed, her teeth bared, her eyes bright, her breasts jiggling. Man, what a sight.

"I already told you I can't. There isn't another room on this floor, and anything else is too far away if Saldana decides to come find you."

She tossed her hair back over her shoulder. "You're here to protect me? Or to lie in wait for Santiago? Am I just bait to you?"

"I'm here to protect you." He was amazed at the calmness of his own voice.

"I told you in Honduras I didn't want your protection. I don't want it now."

"I don't give a damn. If I'm not here, you're going to do something stupid to get that kid back and end up getting yourself killed or under Saldana's thumb again. So, no, I'm not going anywhere."

"I hate you," she said, turning to the bathroom.

"Good."

When she slammed the door, he dropped to the chair and covered his face with his hands. Sure, he was here to keep her from doing something stupid, but who was going to stop him?

Isabella stood under the shower spray, trying not to sob. The damned man would probably hear her and think she was crying over him. He'd be right.

She didn't have the greatest track record with men. She'd

MJ Fredrick

lost her virginity at fourteen to a senior who never spoke to her again. When she recovered from that humiliation, she dipped her toe into the casual-sex scene, but the act always left a bad taste in her mouth, sometimes literally. She'd gone to Honduras with a boy she'd thought she could like, but he'd left her, high and dry, before she found a job as a stripper.

Then she'd met Santiago, and look how that had turned out.

But while she was at his compound, she'd met Eric Reyes. Alex called him Cortez, but in Santiago's house, he'd been Reyes. He'd smiled at her when others ignored her. He'd talked to her, touched her without wanting to screw her. Well, maybe he had, but he hadn't groped, hadn't stared. He'd spoken to her in that soft voice, calling her Bella as Alex sometimes did. She'd felt safe with him and started seeking him out, especially when Santiago was away.

Because of her need to be something more than a whore to a man, he'd died a terrible death.

She'd thought he'd be able to stand up to Santiago's wrath. He had been strong. That just hadn't been enough.

Was Alex? Alex made her feel safe. She thought maybe he could see her as Eric had. But if he only saw her as a whore, as a job—why convince herself otherwise?

She shut off the water, toweled off, realized she hadn't brought her pajamas in here. With a toss of her head, she opened the door and strode out.

Alex was on his side of the bed, watching the news of the upcoming shuttle launch. She walked right in front of the TV, opened the drawer and bent over unnecessarily to retrieve her pajamas.

"You done in there?" he asked, his voice unaffected by the sight of her damp, nude body, and he rolled off the bed in the

132

direction of the bathroom. He stopped at the door, turned to her. "Don't stay up too late. I have a plan for tomorrow."

Chapter Nine

Alex hoped Danes had sent them on the right path when he'd told him Saldana's cousin, the one who laundered his money in Florida, the one whose security guard Bella had tried to seduce, also owned a place in the strip-club district.

Alex offered Isabella a donut as they sat in her little rental car in front of PT's Club. He'd picked up a half dozen on the way. He loved donuts and could easily eat a dozen, but Isabella hadn't eaten anything since—well, he couldn't remember. She hadn't even eaten the chocolate bar he'd brought her last night. He could see the strain on her face, the lost weight. A far cry from the starving woman in the jungle.

"You need to eat something."

She made a face at the donuts. "No thanks."

"You want me to go get breakfast tacos? Sausage biscuits?"

"We might miss something," she said softly, her eyes trained on the building.

"You're not going to be any good to me if you get sick."

"If I eat that, I'll get sick." She nodded toward the sticky box.

"Suit yourself." He sat back, plucked a donut from the box and shoved the whole thing in his mouth, then washed it down with lukewarm coffee. "Could be a long day. I don't think these guys exactly keep bankers' hours."

"I don't want to take any chances."

He opened his mouth to reply, but she shot him a look.

"Do not say anything nice to me. I never know who you are when you say something nice to me."

He lifted his hands in surrender, then licked the glaze off his fingers. "You got it. Kid's gone, you're never going to see him again, all your fault."

"Alex."

"That's what you wanted me to say, right? Feed your guilt?" He leveled a hard glare at her. "Show you what kind of rotten person you are, confirm what you already know."

She shook her head and turned back to the building, her shoulders slumped.

"You're just a stripper, you're not smart enough to do this, no man will ever see past your body, no man will ever know how strong you are. Should I keep going?" he asked when she glanced at him warily, her eyes huge, her face pale.

"I'm not strong."

"I said you weren't. Because no one as weak as you could have made it out of that jungle. Oh, right, I brought you out. You needed me. You need me now. If Santiago finds you before you find him, you would be dead. He won't appreciate you being smart enough to figure out where he is and what he's doing."

"I'm not smart enough," she murmured, turning away again.

"He's hiding, Bella. However he's getting his drugs into this country, he doesn't want to be found."

"How did things come to us? The supplies he ordered?" she asked.

"Near as we can figure, air drops."

"Less likely to happen here," she mused.

"We're looking at ships, which seems most probable, so we have people watching docks."

"Just in Miami?"

He looked at her sharply. "All over Florida."

"Just Florida?"

"What do you know?"

"Nothing. I mean, whatever Eric—Agent Cortez was investigating, do you think it was limited to here? It seems to me it would be easier to get into Texas, across the border, than to come off a ship, unless they were being smuggled. But I'd think ships were more closely watched. The Texas border is long and for the most part unmanned. That's how I would do it," she continued when he just stared. "But I'm just a dumb stripper."

Isabella reached over without looking and took a donut. She started humming something that sounded familiar, but he couldn't place it.

"What's that song? Something you heard last night?"

She smiled, that damn mysterious smile. "A song I used to sing with Hector."

She sang some more, something about colors, in English and Spanish, but the tune still niggled. God knew his mother hadn't sung to him.

"Pretty catchy for a kid's song."

She laughed. "I didn't know a lot of kid songs, you know, I never thought I'd have a baby this young. I couldn't exactly order Disney DVDs. So I made up songs from ones I knew. That one's from the Black Eyed Peas."

Damn, he wanted to see her with that kid, wanted to see what kind of mother she was. Before he could give it more

136

thought, a car pulled up alongside of the building, long and shiny. Three men got out. Two scanned the area as the third straightened his suit jacket and shades.

"That's got to be him," Alex said. "Now what?"

She cinched her top and brushed donut glaze from her lap. "I have an idea."

"No." His tone was sharp, and for the first time, he took his eyes off the sedan. "You're not going in there durring off hours. I can't keep an eye on you."

"I'm just going to apply for a job."

He shook his head, jaw set. "I say we wait."

"Trust me, Alex." She shoved open the door. Straightening, she hitched her jeans down just a little and rolled her hips as she approached the men standing at the door.

Her heart thudded against her ribs as she went over what she would say in her mind. She considered and discarded half a dozen scenarios in the time it took to walk from the car to where the men now stood waiting for her.

"Jorge Medellin?" she asked the man in the middle, the smallest, flanked by two muscular men. Santiago had always kept the company of big men so he could step between them if the going got rough.

"Who's asking?" one of the bodyguards demanded.

"I'm Isabella." She didn't take her eyes from Jorge, but he betrayed no reaction. "I'm looking for Santiago."

Jorge stepped back and gestured toward the door, for her to precede him. She resisted the urge to look back over her shoulder, to get Alex's approval, before she nodded, ducked her head and walked into the darkness.

The scent of stale alcohol, sex and sickness assaulted her the minute she walked in the door. The bar and the three stages, all with poles, were familiar. There was something about this place that made her feel filthy, beyond the three silent men watching her.

She put her hands on her hips, though she wanted to wrap them around herself to hide herself from these men. She tossed her hair and looked up at Jorge.

"Where is he?"

"What makes you think I know?"

"He told me to come here, told me you'd help me hook up with him," she said, thinking on the fly. "I need to find him. I'm running out of money."

"What did you say your name was again?" Jorge leaned against a barstool and looked her over.

She swallowed. She'd told them her real name. What if Santiago had spoken to Jorge about her, for real? What if he dragged her back to Honduras without her son?

"Isabella," she said, not as confidently this time. She hoped using her own name wasn't a mistake. But she was getting desperate now, and perhaps if Santiago knew she was looking for him, he'd show himself.

He reached out to curl her hair around his finger. "What would you want with an old man like Santiago?"

She stumbled mentally. She didn't think of Santiago as old—late forties, maybe. Jorge was definitely not younger, or as well groomed. "I told you, I'm running out of money."

Jorge inclined his head toward the pole on the center stage. "I think I know how a girl like you can earn some cash. You can show us what you have. It's a much easier way to make a living than by answering Santiago's beck and call. I pay very well."

What she wanted, but she needed barriers. She was alone in here with these strangers who made their living off women's bodies. She scrambled for an excuse. "I'm not dressed for it, and I'd really much prefer finding Santiago."

Jorge studied her critically. "Come back tonight."

She blinked. "What?"

"Come back tonight and dance for me. If I like it, I'll tell you what I know about Santiago."

She gritted her teeth, wanting to demand that he tell her now, that every moment counted. But if Jorge was like his cousin, he would never respond to the threats of a woman. Maybe Alex could force him, but could she risk Jorge clamming up because she sicced a Ranger on him?

Could she risk that he was telling her the truth now? That he would tell her something if she stripped for him?

That he even knew anything to tell?

She had to take the chance. "What time do you want me?"

She'd been in there a long time, too long. Alex shoved open the car door and reached for the clutch piece at his ankle. Hell, the minute she'd disappeared behind that door, his skin had started crawling. He didn't want her out of his sight. He definitely didn't want her with that scumbag. What had she been thinking, going behind the door with that man? She would end up back in her Honduran prison.

He checked the area—almost dead this time of day— checked his ammo and got out of the car, edging around the building that fronted the street, moving toward the one set back, the one Isabella had entered.

When he protested this might be to risky, that Santiago might haul her back to Honduras, she'd said she didn't care if Santiago caught her and sent her back, as long as she was with her son. But what kind of life was it for the kid? How long before Santiago started turning the boy against his mother?

She was taking a risk he didn't want her to pay.

Gun at the ready, he headed toward the door, mentally taking in possible places for cover out here—trash can, sign, car, if he could get back to it—trying to picture the place inside. Bar, tables, three guys—maybe more. Who knew what these men were doing here at this hour? It sure as hell looked like they were coming for a meeting.

He reached the door just as it opened and Isabella stepped out. He managed to carry through—instead of aiming the gun at her head, he kept moving and tucked the weapon at the small of his back, flipping his shirt over it to hide it.

She startled, but he motioned her to be quiet and stepped behind the door, out of sight.

Damn, she was a good actress, because if the men behind her hadn't seen her start, they would never know he was here. She looked back at them with a toss of her head.

"I'll see you at ten." She closed the door.

Keeping half his attention on the door and the other on the sashaying form of Isabella making her way to the car—okay, maybe seventy-thirty, and not weighted in the right way—Alex followed her.

Only when he sat beside her did he see her shaking.

"What happens at ten?" He turned the key in the ignition.

"I come back, dance for him, and he tells me what he knows about Santiago." She covered her mouth with a shaking hand, her attention outside the car as they pulled away from the curb.

"Dance? You mean strip?"

She turned dark eyes to him—darker than usual, anyway. "That's what kind of place it is. That's what kind of girl I am."

He wanted to tell her that she wasn't that kind of girl, but he was too pissed. "You didn't think it could be some kind of trap? He tells you to come at ten, he tells Santiago to come at ten, and there you go."

"Of course I thought of that. I'm not as stupid as you think."

Okay, she was defensive.

"How do you know he knows anything?" he asked, swallowing back all the comments he wanted to throw at her for being an idiot.

"I don't. But we don't have anything else, do we?"

"No." Unless O'Malley had turned up something with the credit cards. "I'll call, see if they've found anything from talking to the waitress."

She relaxed a little and nodded as he dialed. O'Malley picked up on the fourth ring.

"Anything on Guillermo Morales?" Alex asked with no preamble.

"The waitress couldn't ID him from pictures, but the credit cards have only been in use for a couple of weeks, which is enough to make us think it's Saldana."

"Still, would he be that arrogant?" Alex asked. "Does he not know we're after him?"

"He's been more cautious in the past," O'Malley admitted. "But we're not taking the chance. We have his spending patterns. Should be able to track him down from this in a matter of hours."

Unease prickled along the back of Alex's neck. Damn, he wanted this to be over but, "He wouldn't be dumb enough to have a spending pattern." He glanced at Isabella for confirmation.

She lifted a shoulder, uncertain.

"We'll know in a few hours," O'Malley said stubbornly.

"Call us," Alex ordered. "As soon as you know one way or another."

O'Malley muttered something that might be agreement, and disconnected. Alex scowled and tossed the phone to the bench seat between them.

"You don't think it's him," she murmured.

"I think you were pretty scared that night. You wanted to see him, wanted to find your son," he amended quickly when she opened her mouth to protest. "I think it's the wrong guy."

She sucked in a sharp breath, and he braced himself for what she might say, but she remained silent. He glanced over to see her staring out the window through her tears.

"You don't have to dance tonight."

"I screwed up with this thing, I need to make it up."

"This is not your job."

She whipped her head around. "Finding my son is my job. No one else will keep looking for him the way I will. If I have to dance to find him, then I will."

It was his turn to suck in a breath. "I'm coming with you."

She shook her head. "How would that look?"

"They won't know I'm with you. They don't know who I am." He hoped. "I'll be in the audience."

She sucked her lower lip between her teeth. "I don't know if that's a good idea."

"What are you talking about? I'll be there to make sure they don't take you anywhere you don't want to go."

"I don't know if I'll be able to dance in front of you." Her voice was muffled behind her hand.

He snorted. "That's what you're worried about? Your stripping ability?"

"You have weird ideas about my body—"

"What, that it should stay covered?"

She glared. "I don't think I can act naturally with you there. I have to be able to convince them to confide in me."

"I'm going to be there," he insisted.

She squeezed her eyes closed. "If Santiago is there, and you catch him, you'll ask him where Hector is first, right? Will you promise me you'll do that?"

He stared straight ahead and resisted the urge to reach for her, to reassure her. All he could do was blow out his breath. "I promise."

Chapter Ten

"What's the signal?" Alex quizzed as she stood in front of the bathroom mirror, layering on eye makeup. In the harsh bathroom light the dark eyeshadow made her look hard, but maybe that was only the determined look in her eyes.

She flicked her gaze to his in the mirror. "Seriously, Alex, I'm not an idiot."

"No, but you've never done this before. You could get nervous. That's not out of the realm of possibility, right?"

She gave her attention back to her mascara. "No, it's not."

"So the signal?"

"I pull on my bra."

"Not the straps, but the band." He inspected the peach-colored lacy garment critically. It cupped her full breasts, but allowed anyone looking to see her dark nipples beneath. "Are you going to take it off?"

"Not if I can get away with not," she said. "I'll have to see what the other girls are doing."

"Because it will be hard to tug on it if some lecherous old guy has it wrapped around his head."

"I know."

"So if Jorge says he's taking you to Santiago or Hector, you tug at the band."

"I know," she said through her teeth, tossing her eyeliner back in her makeup case. "I've got it."

She pushed out the bathroom past him to go to the closet. She pulled out a cream-colored slinky knit dress, inspected it and slipped it on, tying it at her waist like a robe. As far as he could see, that was the only fastening.

"Nervous?"

She scooped her loose hair back from her face. "I haven't danced in four years."

"I'm sure it'll come back to you, easy as riding a pole."

Her body went rigid and she whipped her head around. "Can we call a halt to that? Just for tonight, can't you be on my side?"

Her voice was choked, making him wonder when the last time anyone had been on her side. He nodded once, burying his concern. How come he could trust the men in his company but couldn't bring himself to trust her?

"I don't like this plan. It's needlessly risky."

"Noted." She slipped her bare feet into incredibly high strappy sandals.

"Bella—"

"You can get back to me on this when someone you love is missing," she said sharply. "Now, this is hard enough without me having to worry about you. Are you going to take me or not?"

Something in her voice had him reaching for her, curling his fingers into a fist and withdrawing before he said, "What you're doing—it's very brave."

"I'll do anything to get my son back," was all she said.

He stepped back, toward the door. "Let's go."

She was silent on the ride over, but gave him a small smile

145

before climbing out of the truck to go into the bar. Alex hung back, waited about fifteen minutes before he followed. They were the longest fifteen minutes, unable to track her and what trouble she could be getting into.

He paid his cover and passed through the metal detector. When he walked into the club, dark except for the lights around the bar and the spotlights on the stage, he scanned quickly for danger, aware that he was being scanned as well. He noted Julian in one corner, looking disreputable with a scruffy beard and Dave in a seat by the right stage, across the room from Julian. Dave had let his hair grow, so he didn't look as military as Alex. Sergeant Major Danes was at the bar.

Jorge was nowhere in sight. Alex hoped he wasn't in the back harassing Isabella. He hoped he wasn't in the back doing anything else to her, either.

No, Isabella wouldn't sleep with Jorge without knowing he had information. At least, Alex hoped she wasn't that desperate.

He scanned the stages. Three women danced, but none could hold a candle to Isabella.

What the hell was wrong with him that he was comparing strippers to her?

Alex walked to the bar, every nerve alert. He ordered a beer from the overweight shaggy bartender who passed him the bottle and didn't even look up. Alex paid and turned back toward the stage, tilting the bottle so the liquid cooled his throat. The beer did nothing to ease the knot in his stomach. Damn, he hadn't been this nervous about an operation in years, but he'd never had a civilian involved before.

He didn't want to choose a table till he knew which stage Isabella would be dancing on.

A stick girl wandered off stage and the pulsing of a Black Eyed Peas song began. Alex took a seat at the edge of the middle stage when Isabella strode from behind the curtains. With a flip of her hair and a flick of her wrist, her dress dropped away, no preamble. She wrapped both hands around the pole and did a twirl, rolling her hips clad in those lace panties. To his left, he heard a wolf whistle and felt heat rise in a surge of protectiveness. She dropped till her ass touched her heels, her body still circling the metal pole. With a display of unsuspected athleticism, she lifted herself and faced the audience, her body undulating, her breasts, so damn high in that bra, nearly touching the pole. On his right, a man groaned and Alex clenched a fist.

As if she knew how crazy the action would make him, she started making her rounds of the stage, shaking her tits at that one, her ass at another, holding still only long enough for them to tuck ratty dollar bills into her thong with their grubby fingers.

He hated this. He hated the overwhelming urge to snatch her off the stage and wrap her back in that dress. Haul her out of here. He ground his teeth together so hard he couldn't even hear the music anymore.

Then she was in front of him, legs straight, palms on her thighs, and bent forward. Her cleavage was deep, sexy as hell, but his gaze was drawn to her knowing eyes. Keeping his gaze on hers, he tucked a bill between her breasts, careful not to touch her smooth skin.

A flick of her eyes and then she rose, twirling, undulating, turning her back to the pole and sliding down it, her knees falling apart, opening herself up to him, sliding her hands down her thighs and back up again, drawing attention to what was his.

The thought was strong, surprising him, tensing every muscle in his body in fight mode. Only the person he wanted to fight was himself.

God, she was stunning, and arousing, and she was dancing for him now, turning her back, bending over almost to the floor, her ass in the air. He wanted to glide his hands over the curves there, over her thighs, wanted to bend over her and nip her throat as he plunged into her. He indulged himself in the fantasy, was aided when she turned her head to look back at him, hair tumbling over one shoulder, eyes telling him she knew what he was thinking.

With a snap of her back and her neck, she ended the song with a flourish, to raucous applause. She smiled and spun on the ball of her foot, dipped to snatch up her dress before she disappeared behind the curtain.

Christ. He struggled to keep his expression neutral, preferring to focus on that than on the conflict of arousal and protectiveness.

She emerged from behind the curtain with a swagger. She didn't look at him, avoided the touch of her admirers with skill, and walked over behind a curtained area at the opposite end of the room from the door.

Crap, why hadn't he gone to look over there? Of course Jorge would be all Wizard of Oz, segregated from the general clientele but with a clear view of the stage. No telling who was with him.

Alex started to rise, but met Julian's eyes. The younger man shook his head and leaned back in his chair, showing Alex he had a better vantage point without drawing as much attention.

Didn't matter. Tension ran through Alex's nerves like live wires. She was only behind the curtain, but she may as well have been behind a brick wall. And he had nothing to protect her.

Minutes passed, then more minutes. Alex's gut tightened painfully. Making his decision, he pushed to his feet and went over, ignoring Julian's glare. He stumbled on purpose, playing the drunk, and ducked behind the curtain.

Sitting at a semicircular table, Isabella was snuggled up against Jorge. She looked up sharply when Alex staggered back, and he saw the panic in her eyes, followed by an expression that assured him she had everything under control.

What it looked like she had was her hand on Jorge's lap.

"Sorry, man. Trying to find the bathroom," he muttered.

Jorge pointed through the sheer curtain to a giant neon sign behind the right stage.

"Dude, sorry." He gave Isabella a long look, then headed off. Walking away was hard, so he turned back. "Great dance," he said, and turned away.

He continued his drunk act into the bathroom, where Danes joined him.

"Smooth," the older man said.

Alex shook off the criticism. "I had to see who was back there."

"What she was doing?"

"Nah, that—she's doing what she has to do." He tightened his jaw, because he had expected to see her bartering for information with her body. He still wasn't sure what he would have done if she had been.

Danes rested a hip against the sink. "Don't try to kid me, man. You didn't blink when she was on that stage."

"Did you?" Alex challenged.

The older man snorted and turned to wash his hands. "She's gorgeous, sure, but that wasn't why you were watching her. Why you were determined to see who she was with."

"I'm not—"

"You're attached." Danes dried his hands and folded massive arms over his barrel chest. "Happens sometimes when you're in each other's pockets. Can't let it get to you."

"It's not."

Danes gave him a look that told Alex he'd been there, lied the same lies. "Right. Just watch yourself. This assignment will be over, and then what? Will you really know who she is?"

Would he? Did he want to?

He walked out of the restroom in time to see Isabella emerge from behind the curtain, Jorge touching her arm. He leaned over to brush a kiss across her cheek. Isabella gave him a charming smile and turned away.

Alex strode toward the door, anxious to be out of here, but not wanting to appear to leave with her. He reached the door just as she did. She gave him the same smile she'd given Jorge and dipped her head, walking past him as he held the door for her. Once outside, they headed in opposite directions, she to the corner, he to the truck. He drove around the block to meet her so they wouldn't be followed. She climbed silently into the car.

"What did you find out?"

She shook her head, not looking at him.

"He didn't know anything?" Alex demanded, angry at the humiliation she'd had to endure for nothing.

"He said Santiago has gone to Texas. He didn't know anything about Hector." Her voice was distant, tired. Dejected.

Shock jolted him. "You asked him about Hector?" That had not been part of the plan. She was a woman seeking a protector. Revealing she was a mother could hurt her chances.

"Not directly. But he didn't know anything about Santiago

traveling with anyone."

"Do you think Jorge knows what he's talking about?" Alex hated the impatience coloring his voice, but damn, she'd risked everything for very little return. The way she was acting, this ghost of the Isabella he knew, was scaring the crap out of him.

"What did you think he'd tell me? I am just a stripper, you know." She shifted in her seat toward him. "Speaking of, you appeared to enjoy my dance."

He choked. "Yeah, well, you weren't as rusty as you thought."

"I guess not." She gave him one of those twisty little smiles that hit him right in the gut.

He slammed the door on the image that smile brought to mind. "What did Jorge think?"

"He thought I fulfilled his expectations."

"Is that what you were doing with your hand under the table when I came back there?"

She stiffened. "No."

"Look, I know you'd do anything to get information about Hector—"

"I didn't, Alex." Her voice was tight, almost on the verge of tears.

"You don't have to answer to me. Like you said, I don't know what you're going through, what you'd do to change what's happened. I'm in no position to judge."

"Yet that doesn't stop you."

He didn't say anything as he checked the rearview mirror. He couldn't let his frustration with Isabella get them in trouble because he wasn't paying attention.

"I made him think I was going to," she said when they turned onto the highway. "But I didn't want to seem too desperate. I figured it was better to leave him wanting."

"So you're going to see him again?"

"No. But I made him think I was."

"He doesn't know where you're staying."

"Of course not."

"But he knows who you are to Santiago?"

He couldn't shake the feeling that the night had been a trap. For Jorge to part with the information, for him to let her go.

"No. I mean, he doesn't know Santiago was holding me down in Honduras. He doesn't know I'm the mother of his child. He just thinks Santiago is my sugar daddy."

Alex frowned. "I don't trust him."

She saw him glance in the rearview mirror and twisted to look behind them. "Are they after us?"

"No. Not that I can tell."

She turned back and leaned her head against the seat with a sigh. "Thanks. For being there."

"What?"

"I wasn't as scared as I thought I would be. I knew you were there if I needed you. Thank you."

"This isn't the first time."

"Well, it's the first time I'm saying thank you. So take it."

"All right, got it. Jesus."

"Alex."

He slid her a look and she reached across the cab to lay a light hand on his lap, determined he would understand her meaning.

He did, because he went all stiff, and not just in the good way. "Don't," he said through his teeth.

152

"I know you were aroused back there. You forget I know you. I can see in your eyes when you want me. I wanted you to want me."

"So you can fuck with my head?"

"Not really what I want to fuck with."

"Why? You need your release?"

"Maybe."

She turned in her seat then, shifted her touch to cover his erection. He growled her name and swerved, just a little, when she squeezed. Then she released him long enough to unzip him.

"Not here," Alex said, pushing her away, his resistance melting as he zipped himself up. He wasn't made of steel. Steel-like at the moment, though.

He made the drive more quickly, tense, silent. He passed his keys to the valet and followed Isabella into the lobby. She didn't look back, but he could tell by the swing of her hips, the tension in the cab of the truck, what was on her mind.

The elevator opened as they approached, like the answer to a prayer, and he swept her inside. The doors slid closed with no one else getting on. Winding her arms around his neck, she gave a soft purr against his mouth. Sliding his touch down to her bare thigh, he eased her against the wall as he sought her taste with his tongue, her soft skin with his rough hands. She lifted one leg along his thigh, rubbing lightly. Needing to be closer, he pressed into her, angling his mouth for a deeper taste. He scooped her hair back from her face and rested his palm against her smooth cheek. Longing swamped him and he let her kiss carry him deeper.

The ringing of the elevator echoed in his head a moment before he realized what it was, and he moved back from Isabella. She opened her eyes slowly, lips parted as if she was savoring the last of the kiss.

He didn't want to see realization snap back into her eyes, not yet. He took her hand and stepped into the hall. When the elevator doors thumped shut, he dragged her close to kiss her again.

And ignored the flash of hope he saw in her eyes.

"Alex," she whispered.

"Hush."

She gasped when he nipped her lower lip between his teeth, then slid his tongue over it. His name was a plea against his mouth, and he dipped his tongue between her lips. His fingers tangled in her hair for a minute, released, and he moved back, trying to remember which way the room was.

"Here," she said, apparently seeing his confusion and tugging his hand.

With trembling fingers, she pulled out her key card, turned toward a door—God, he hoped it was the right one—and he crowded her against it, nuzzling her throat through her hair, pressing his erection against her ass.

She laughed his name and shoved open the door. They stumbled in together. He pushed her hair out of the way to get to the skin of her throat, salty and musky.

So fucking sexy.

She stepped out of her heels as he turned her, and was suddenly tiny. Clasping her rib cage under her breasts, he raised her on her toes to bring her closer and bent to deepen the kiss. She wound around him, arms, legs, as he held the heat of her over his erection. Her breath came hot and heavy as she worked the buttons of his shirt. Shaking with the desire to feel her beneath him, he dropped her to the bed, following her down, nestling between her thighs.

Willpower kicked in. He had to slow down, had to ease

back. This wouldn't be like last time. He would make her see he was different than the other men. He would make her understand it was about more than release.

If he could hold out, he would make her as crazy as he was. He rose on his knees and loosened her dress, parting it to bare the sexy underwear.

Mine.

The thought was so loud in his head that he jolted, but Bella rolled her hips, drawing his attention back.

"You're the most beautiful woman I've ever seen," he murmured, sliding his fingertips from the base of her throat, between her breasts, over her belly and the triangle of lace, to rest on her thigh.

"Alex." She sat up and took his face between her palms, brushing her thumbs over his stubble, and then kissed him, her mouth hot and mobile, her legs parting around him on the bed.

Her eagerness played havoc with his vow to take his time. He tilted her back on the bed and lowered his head.

Chapter Eleven

Isabella parted her lips for his kiss. This wasn't a lip-crusher, one of those kisses that told her he wanted her but that he hated the wanting. This one was—not soft, because nothing about Alex was soft, but tender, just a shadow of the overwhelming desire she'd received from him before. He brushed his fingertips over her cheek, so lightly the caress sent tremors through her.

He smiled against her and shifted, pressing her into the pillow, slanting his mouth over hers and just—kissing her. She hummed in the back of her throat, needing to discharge the energy spinning through her.

She stroked her fingers over his hair, the soft prickle of it adding another dimension, another layer of sensation to the slow, dreamy kiss.

His breath feathered against her cheek, the pulse of his heart against her arm as he rolled his tongue along hers.

Still he didn't touch her, only kissed her. The last time she'd just kissed a boy had been when she didn't know any better, didn't know where these sensations could lead. Didn't know that sex was about control. Learned that she could be the one in control.

Except with Alex. God, what was he doing to her? Was he trying to forge a deeper connection, stronger than she had

Breaking Daylight

already? Didn't he understand how hard she'd worked to put her guard in place?

"Alex—"

"Shh." He eased his lips along her jaw, then back up to her chin and down the line of her throat.

Even her fingers spasmed with pleasure as he brushed his stubble over sensitive nerves. "Can't." She said the word on a shuddering breath.

He palmed her jaw, turned her head to the side for better access to her throat. "Smell good," he said.

When he touched his tongue to the area below her ear, her body heated, and she arched toward him, encouraging his touch. Instead he kissed her again, slowly, tasting every crevice of her mouth until her blood buzzed, her breathing sped up, her hands moved over his face and shoulders, without thinking.

It would hurt, yes, when he left her, if she opened herself to him this way. But she wasn't backing away from this chance to be cherished. To be seduced.

He stroked her back and circled his fingers lazily, sending her tingling nerves directly where she needed his touch. She whispered his name, not a protest this time, and slid her leg along his. He applied only the slightest pressure at the small of her back, drawing her closer against his body.

He was warm and smelled so good, musky with that hint of soap beneath. His erection pressed against her through his boxers, and she teased him with her proximity, back and forth, until his breath became as ragged as hers. He rose over her, not taking his eyes from her as he dragged his fingers down her chest. She lay breathless, boneless, when he lowered his mouth to her skin, starting at the hollow of her throat and moving down, a combination of soft, firm lips and scratchy stubble. The moan pushed its way past her tongue, filled the room, vibrated

157

the bed, and she gripped the back of his head as he shoved aside the lace cup and nuzzled her naked breast. Desire twinged through her, almost painful, as he plucked her nipple with his lips before settling into a deeper caress, a worshipful one, his hands on either side of her body.

Then, with a gentle bite to the underside of her breast, he slid his fingers into her thong. But instead of pushing her panties down, he closed his palms over her ass and lifted.

Languorous with what he'd been doing, she didn't understand that he meant her to turn over. Of course, he was an ass man, he would want her in that position. She hated the stab of disappointment. Up till now it had seemed to be about her. Slowly she turned and shuddered with pleasure when he framed her thighs between his arms and blew across her naked skin. He chuckled at the gooseflesh he raised, then bent to kiss her spine at the small of her back, his caress just as careful, as worshipful, as his kisses to her mouth had been.

Her nerve endings exploded in quick bursts as pleasure shot out from each contact of his mouth, his chin. He slid his hands up her thighs and down again, without touching her, without caressing her swelling flesh, her body desperate for him.

"Alex, please."

He nipped the curve of her ass and rose. She braced herself for his thrust, but instead he brushed his thumbs over the sensitive flesh where her buttocks met her thighs, and the wash of desire was so powerful she dropped her head back to the pillow.

"Don't get comfortable," he said and turned her onto her back with a flop, pulling down her thong. "I want to watch you."

Suddenly she wished he'd taken her in the other position. What would he see in her face when he entered her, when he made her come? Would she be able to school herself against showing him too much, giving him too much power?

He sheathed and positioned himself at her entrance, watching her as he slowly pushed into her.

Desire radiated from every nerve he pressed against as he entered her. She arched her head back but he stopped and cupped her face in his palms.

"Watch me."

She never thought looking into a man's eyes—into Alex's eyes—would be so hard, watching the flicker of emotions that only deepened her own, the longing, the pleasure, the need. She gasped as he filled her, then began to move. She wanted to close her eyes against it, to protect herself, to bring that wall back between them, but he challenged her as he moved over her, caressing her body with gentle strokes that only stoked the desire he'd already built. Keeping the same rhythm, he grasped her ass.

She shattered, was only vaguely aware of his urge for her to look at him, until he enfolded her in his arms, lifted her onto his thighs, still thrusting. Unable to hold her head up, she met his gaze, watched his eyes darken, deepen, heard the catch of his breath. She tucked her head against his shoulder as he gathered her close, shuddering with his own release.

He pulled out of her, but they stayed in the same position, as if moving would reveal something more of themselves than they'd already done. Finally, she slid sideways off him, not looking at him, gathering her dress.

What had they done? How could she face him after being so vulnerable in front of him?

She turned toward him, wiping her hair from her eyes with the back of her hand. She would not cover her nakedness, would not give him that satisfaction.

Alex watched the play of emotions over her face, none of them the gratitude he thought he'd see. Hell, she looked scared, and pissed because of it. He opened his mouth to ask her what the hell was wrong when his phone rang.

He swore and dove for it, digging it out of his discarded pants. Bella took advantage of his distraction to head toward the bathroom, but her curiosity must've got the better of her, because she hesitated in the doorway and watched as he answered.

"Yeah?"

"Get your rocks off?"

Alex scowled. Who the hell? While he was working on who it was on the other end, the voice continued.

"Turn on your TV."

Danes. Christ. "What the hell, Lionel? You scared the shit out of me." He reached over and turned on the TV, aware Isabella had walked back into the room, her attention on the TV.

There, on the news, was video of a fire. Alex couldn't place it at first, though it was familiar.

"Jorge's club," Isabella murmured, clutching her dress in front of her. "We were just there."

"And just missed the shit," Lionel said. "You two left, some guys came in with guns, looking for Isabella. Chased out most of the people, put some bullets in anyone who tried to stop them, including the bartender who drew on them. Not sure if they meant to set the place on fire, but it damn sure went up fast."

"Christ. Are you hurt? Julian? Dave?"

"All got out by playing perverts instead of heroes."

Alex could hear the disgust in the sergeant major's voice.

"Who died?"

"Don't know. I stayed outside till the ambulances started carrying out bodies. Jorge was one. Looked like the fire got him, along with any of his men who rushed to his aid. One of the girls."

Alex's stomach rolled. It could have been Isabella. He studied the screen, looking for any familiar face. Isabella slipped on her dress and sat beside him, leaning forward, doing the same.

"Did you get a look at them?" Alex asked, reaching behind him for his boxers.

"Big Hispanics carrying cannons," Lionel said dismissively. "Not out of the ordinary. Except—shit."

The screen flickered for an instant to show Alex and Isabella in the elevator, in the hall, him pressed up against her, his hands all over her. Alex sat forward.

"What the hell? Where are you?"

"Security," Lionel said. "I was entertaining myself waiting for the two of you to finish. I gave you enough time, I hope?"

"Why are you in security?" How had he wired it to the TV in their room? Hell, how did he know which room was theirs? Which hotel they were in?

"Watching for these guys." The screen flipped again as three big Hispanics who looked like they were carrying came through the lobby doors.

Alex swore. "Get dressed," he ordered Isabella quietly. "They're not on tape too, are they?" he demanded into the phone when Isabella burst into action, yanking open drawers before turning to pick up the room phone. He was about to yell at her when he heard her ask for the valet to bring his truck around. Smart girl.

"Not on tape. You better hurry. Call me when you get out."

Alex stood and pulled on his boxers with one hand while folding his phone closed with the other. He watched as Isabella shrugged the loose dress off and tugged on her underwear as she dashed to the closet.

"Something you can run in," Alex said, kicking aside the heels she'd been wearing earlier.

She ripped jeans off a hanger and stumbled into them while he whipped his shirt over his head and started throwing clothes into his duffel. She twisted her way into the jeans and a snug T-shirt, then grabbed clothes from the hook, tossed them at him and ran into the bathroom.

"No time for your makeup," he muttered.

She threw their toothbrushes into her purse and scowled. She shoved her feet into some wedge-heeled things and grabbed her purse and the key card.

"Are you kidding me?" Alex finished lacing his own shoes and stood, looking pointedly at her feet.

"They're the most practical things I have."

"God help us." He shoved his gun into the front pocket of his cargo pants and hefted the duffel. "Go. Stairs."

"Won't they expect that?"

"They don't know we know they're coming." God, he hoped. "Element of surprise."

She raced down the hall toward the stairway door, but he stepped in front of her before she could open it.

"Just in case," he muttered and pushed open the door that made too much noise. He checked the stairwell, then glanced over his shoulder at the elevator bank before ushering her ahead of him.

She headed down the first flight, grasping the rail,

stumbled on the second flight, snatched off her shoes while she was still moving and continued down barefoot.

She started breathing heavily around the fifth flight, coughing at the sixth.

Ten more to go. Shit.

"Just—my breath—a second," she panted, leaning over the rail. She looked down, groaned, and stepped away from the rail.

Above them, a door opened and closed like a damned alarm.

"No time," he muttered, grabbed her arm and started hauling her down the stairs so her feet struggled to keep up.

"Alex," she protested and started coughing again.

He touched his fingertip to her mouth when he heard footsteps quicken on the stairs above them. Fuck. He rounded the staircase to the next exit door, shoved it open and pushed her out onto the carpeted hallway.

"Where?" she asked breathlessly.

He wished he could trust the elevator. Instead, he dragged her to the other end of the hall, the other stairwell, pressing the elevator buttons as he passed. Hopefully the men following them would think they'd taken the elevator.

He entered the other stairway cautiously, then fished out his phone, Isabella still plastered to his side. He could feel her heart trying to beat its way out of her chest.

"Where are they?" he asked Lionel without preamble, presuming the man was still in the security booth.

"Ninth floor," the older man said. "They've split. One went into the elevators, one went down the stairs."

"There were three," Alex said.

"I don't see the third guy, and I don't know how long I can stay here."

"Yeah, I get it," Alex said. "I'll call you when we're out." If they got out. He flipped the phone closed without waiting for an answer. Nine flights. Shit. They were bound to figure out this stairwell soon.

"How's your balance?" he asked Isabella, eyeing the rail.

"You're kidding."

"You want to run the rest of the way?"

She looked down into the stairwell and swallowed hard. "I don't know."

"Try." It wasn't a suggestion.

She climbed up to sit on the rail, clutching her shoes and purse to her chest. She slid down a bit, then caught herself with a soft cry of surprise. Before he could chide her, she let go and slid to the bottom of the flight. She staggered a bit when she landed, but went to the next rail and did it again.

When he caught up to her three flights later, she was flushed and suppressing nervous giggles, but her heart thundered beneath his touch. He could see her pulse bouncing in her throat.

"Okay?" he asked.

She nodded and went again, him right behind her.

A door opened above them, one floor up. Isabella looked at him and whipped down the next rail, rubbing her ass before she jumped on the next. Yeah, a little friction did a lot to heat up the jeans.

When he felt they had enough room between them and whoever else was on the stairs—whoever it was didn't seem in much of a hurry—he caught Isabella's hand and they started running again.

Three more floors, two, one, the lobby.

He pushed her behind the door and drew his gun discreetly

before opening the door to peer out into the open space between here and the door.

Not a lot of people this late at night, but he didn't have the best vantage point. His target—or targets, they may have reunited—could be anywhere between here and the valet stand. With no one around, he and Isabella wouldn't exactly be inconspicuous. Damn if he wanted to have a firefight in the middle of a hotel in downtown Miami.

"Stay here," he said to her quietly. "When I get to the truck, I'll signal you."

"What about him?" she asked, pointing to the determined footsteps overhead.

"When you see his feet, bolt. But not before then. Can you keep an eye on both of us?"

She nodded. "Be safe," she whispered.

He glanced over. Her eyes were huge, fear gleaming in them. He leaned over, pressed a hard kiss to her mouth and stepped into the lobby, gun hand hidden behind his duffel.

Chapter Twelve

Spots appeared before Isabella's eyes before she realized she'd forgotten to breathe. She strained to hear descending footsteps, watching for Alex's signal. Would they make it out of here? She needed to feel the tension leave her body, to feel her heart return to normal.

Her heart rate hadn't been normal since Alex had kissed her in the elevator.

Okay, since she danced just for him.

Would her heart ever be normal again?

She watched him cross the lobby, his stride confident, a man on a mission, a man afraid of nothing. But she recognized the minute he saw the enemy, saw the line of his shoulders tighten, saw him nod to someone she couldn't see, behind a pillar. She wished he'd taken her with him. She felt completely vulnerable here.

He looked over and motioned to her. She burst out of the door just as she saw the feet of her pursuer out of the corner of her eye. Racing barefoot across the lobby, she joined Alex at the valet stand, where he got his keys as if he had all the time in the world. He tipped the valet and they stepped out onto the driveway, where the truck waited.

Now he was a blur of motion, opening the door for her. She vaulted in while he walked around the front, tossed the duffel between them and put the car in gear. Behind them, hurrying footsteps raced out onto the driveway.

"Get down," he commanded, and swung the car onto the road.

She dropped to the floorboard, facing the seat, and clung to it as he whipped the truck left, then right, so the vehicle swayed on its shocks. Alex glanced in the rearview mirror repeatedly, his jaw tight, but everything else about him relaxed.

In his element.

"What now?" she asked.

"We make sure they're not behind us, then we call Lionel."

"Are they behind us?"

"Can't tell. Two cabs pulled out after us, but they don't seem to be in a hurry to catch up."

"They don't need to be. This isn't the movies. They just need to know where we're going."

He glanced at her, then accelerated. His face was grim when he looked in the rearview mirror. He turned, then turned again. Nausea welled up in her as she held onto the seat and the doorway, her spine bumping the glove box. She hated not being able to see where she was going, just like when they'd dropped off the cliff in the jungle. But she stifled that. She would not give him something else to worry about. She manned up and held on.

His phone rang. Isabella jolted, Alex swore, then dug the phone out of his breast pocket and tossed it to Isabella. She stared at it a moment.

"Open it," he snapped.

She did and held it to her ear.

"Are you going to make me chase you all the way to Texas?" the gruff voice demanded.

"Who is this?" she asked, her voice high and tight to her own ears.

"Danes. The one who made sure those assholes didn't follow you. Let me talk to Alex."

She lifted the phone to Alex, who scowled. "It's Danes," she said. "He's following us."

Alex looked in the rearview mirror again before he took the phone. "Yeah?"

"Pull over, Shepard."

"Where?"

"That McDonald's looks good."

Alex made a sharp right. He flipped the phone closed and tossed it on the seat in front of Isabella. "Stay there." He shoved open the door, alert, ready to draw his gun.

A cab pulled into the lot behind them. Alex tensed as the back door opened. Beyond him, she saw the big man step out and cast Alex a chiding look.

Alex glanced at Isabella and dropped his hand away from his gun. "You can come out."

She rose slowly from the floorboards, not realizing how tight she'd been curled up until she had to force her muscles to relax. She unfolded herself from the truck and stood by Alex on shaking legs. She didn't fail to notice that he angled himself between her and Danes. Did he not trust this man?

Realization hit hard. Did he trust anyone?

"They didn't follow?"

"I made sure they couldn't," Danes said in his rough voice. "The next step is to get you out of town. I have a hunting cabin near the Everglades. There's a Walmart on the way, you can get the girl some shoes." He gestured to her bare feet.

"We can't leave town," Isabella protested, her voice shrill. "I have to find my son."

Danes pointed a scolding finger at her. "Young lady, those men were there to kill you, to kill both of you, like they killed those others in the fire tonight. You won't find the kid if you're dead."

"We also won't find him if we're hiding." She whirled on Alex. "You promised you'd help me find him."

"I will."

He looked exhausted, the circles beneath his eyes dark, strain tightening his body. Strain she'd caused him because he was protecting her.

"I'll have my men on it," he continued. "But it makes sense for us to lay low. We don't even know where to look."

"Texas, Jorge said." She recognized the desperation in her own voice.

He sighed. "Yeah, well, Texas is a big state. Just a couple of days. Lionel can leave a trail for them to follow, and when the heat is off, we'll look again. By then, we may have a better idea where."

"We must have been getting close for them to be trying to kill us." The idea terrified her. She'd been prepared for Santiago to take her back. She didn't want to think what would happen to her son if Santiago killed her.

Alex and Lionel exchanged looks. What did *that* mean? She curled her fingers into fists and resisted the urge to slug Alex's arm. That would be childish. He'd just risked his life for her, after all.

"Give the master sergeant your credit card, he'll use it, heading toward Texas. They'll follow that trail, and not us."

She turned back and dug into her purse. She might have just run away from her chance to find Hector. She sat on the floorboard of the driver's side of the truck, her feet barely reaching the asphalt of the parking lot, trembling with frustration and fear. Would she ever reunite with Hector?

Alex stepped toward the tailgate of the truck, talking low with Lionel, who passed him something, then turned back to the cab.

Alex returned to the driver's side door and looked down at her. "Get in. I'll get you something to eat, you'll feel better."

She crawled over to her side silently. What choice did she have? She'd never find Hector on her own, and even if she did, how would she get him away from Santiago?

He started the car and pulled through the drive-through of the McDonald's. "What do you want?" he asked, his voice flat.

"Doesn't matter."

He stared at her a minute. "You need protein," he decided and ordered a selection from the menu.

Only when he pulled the bag in and scents filled the car did she realize how hungry she was. He sucked on his shake as he pulled back onto the road and she dug into the fries.

As they headed out of town, the only words they exchanged were "Dig out my burger," and "Is there any ketchup?"

The tension eased out of her body and helplessness took its place. She stared out the window at the passing city and wondered where her child could be. Was it even possible to find him? The probability seemed overwhelmingly against them.

They stopped at a Walmart on the edge of town. They split up and met back at the register. Alex checked the Keds she'd picked up with a scowl, which deepened when he saw the three thick romance novels in her basket.

"You still need your goddamn white knights? We're living on my money now," he said.

"I have cash," she retorted, pulling her basket back defensively. "I need them."

He rolled his eyes and turned to put his products on the belt. Canned meat, canned vegetables, toilet paper, Nutri-Grain bars, packaged fruit, bottled water, new boxers. Practical.

Condoms. A dozen.

She looked from the box to him. "I don't know what you're going to be doing, but I'm going to be reading."

"In case the opportunity comes up. Wouldn't do to be caught without."

"Boy Scout," she muttered. In retaliation, she grabbed two bags of chips, two jars of dip, two Diet Cokes and five candy bars and threw them in her basket. He didn't even blink when she unloaded her products.

She did wince when the total took more of a chunk out of her cash than she expected. He grinned as he hefted her bags as well as his to cart to the truck.

"Gotta be careful," he said on the way out. "We don't know how long we'll be without a cash flow." He loaded the bags with the cans and the bottled water into the back of the truck, tossed the rest under her feet in the cab. "Even when you get Hector back, you gotta think of what you're going to do next. Won't be easy getting a job."

"No." She hadn't thought that far ahead.

"What kind of thing were you looking at?"

Now he wanted to talk? Was he trying to guarantee that he would use some of those condoms and the price wouldn't be wasted?

"I don't know. I don't exactly have a lot of qualifications. I didn't finish college, I've only had one job."

"Which you don't want to do with a kid."

171

"Which I may have to."

"When he finds out what you are? Then what?"

She hated even thinking that he was right. She didn't want a job she'd have to hide from her child, and she didn't want a job where she'd leave him at night, not in the long run. But maybe for now. "He's young, Alex."

"You think you can hide it from him."

"I can make a good living at it. Just tonight I made sixty bucks, with one dance."

"Twenty of that was mine."

Anger snapped her head up. "You want it back?"

"I'm just saying. You need to get a real job."

She couldn't think of that now. She shoved her hair back from her face. "Let me get through one thing at a time."

"No way to live your life if you have a kid."

"Yeah, well, it's the only way I know how to do it."

The cabin, an hour and a half away from any civilization, was a glorified single-wide trailer, flat roofed with a screened-in porch built onto the front, filled with fishing accessories, including a canoe. The whole place smelled of fish and mildew, overlying a lingering scent of burnt cooking oil. Alex turned on the light as they walked into the kitchenette. The counter was cluttered with dishes—clean, at least—and a line of dead ants. Bleh. Alex put their Walmart bags on the linoleum table.

She reached over to crank open a window to get the smell out, but Alex stopped her, pointing to a hole in the screen the size of a quarter.

"We'll get eaten alive."

"Well, see if any windows have good screens. I can't stand

the smell." She looked at him. "Doesn't it bother you?"

"I've smelled worse." He made his way toward the bathroom, opened the door and jerked his head back. "Okay, maybe not. Christ." He stepped in, and she heard him running water in the tub, felt the vibration of the water hitting the fiberglass through the floorboards. Then he flushed the toilet and swore more. "I don't think he uses the tub to bathe," he muttered. "But I did get a window open in there."

"God." She dreaded the bedroom but followed him down the narrow hall.

"It's the carpet you smell," he said. "Gets damp, he comes tramping in from fishing. Not pleasant, but not like a dead body or anything." He turned on the light in the bedroom.

She looked around his shoulder. "You may as well take those condoms back because I am not getting naked in that."

"We should have brought our own sheets," he agreed, eyeing the polyester bedspread with spots of mildew on the corner. The pillows were flat and yellowed, with no cases.

"And disinfectant spray." Isabella turned to look in the cabinets around the small room, where she found thin towels. "We can cover the pillows with these."

"The sheets aren't too bad," Alex said after ripping the covers back to the end of the bed. He dropped onto the mattress that didn't so much as bounce, and lay back. "Hell, I'm so tired I could sleep on the carpet."

She inspected the screens around the room, found two that were secure enough that she felt safe opening the window, and the small trailer was filled with sounds of wilderness, different from the ones in Honduras. Of course, she hadn't opened the windows there, Santiago never would have allowed it.

She carried the thin towels to the bed and sat beside Alex. His eyes were closed, his arm thrown over his eyes, but she knew he wasn't asleep yet.

Outside she heard a rumbling growl, followed by a kind of bark. She jolted and moved closer to Alex.

"What is that?"

"Alligator."

She whipped her head around to stare at him, grabbing his hand in panic, then looked past him out the window. "Are you kidding me?"

Lazily he laced his fingers through hers. "Bull. Mating call."

"How on earth do you know that?"

"Have them in North Carolina. Don't worry. It won't come in."

"I won't go out." Ever. "So what now?"

He shook his head, arm still crooked over his face. "I haven't figured that out yet."

She opened her mouth to press, but sensed his exhaustion and frustration, so instead asked, "The tub is pretty disgusting?"

"Whole bathroom is," he muttered, eyes still closed.

With a sigh, she pushed herself off the bed. She found a worn washcloth and towel, took Alex's toilet paper from the bag and headed in.

The toilet had a black ring at the water level, the tub was grimy, but the sink was relatively clean. She ran warm water and stripped to her underwear, careful not to let her clothes touch the floor—no telling when they'd be able to wash, and she didn't want to carry this smell around with them.

With the hand soap, she cleaned quickly. She could still smell Alex on her. God, so much had happened since they'd made love, and that had only been a few hours ago. She washed his scent off, washed her feet and rinsed. Walking on top of her shoes, she made her way naked back into the bedroom, where Alex was on his side, toward the open window, asleep. She tugged his duffel open, found her kitten pajamas and slipped them on. Only once she was dressed and on the bed beside Alex, did she start to cry.

The heavy weight of Alex's arm across her waist woke her. She had no idea what time it was, if it was dark because of the time or because they were surrounded by trees. Alex's breath was even, warm on the back of her neck. She'd never slept with a man all night, other than Alex, and even then he hadn't touched her in his sleep, as if he'd had to keep his guard up.

Why had he let his guard down now?

She turned onto her back. She couldn't see him but stroked his stubbled jaw. His breathing stuttered, evened out. Awake or asleep? Preferring to think he was asleep, she continued her exploration, gliding her touch down his chest.

She cupped him through his pants. He caught his breath, definitely awake now, heavy and warm against her palm.

"Bella," he murmured, but it wasn't a protest.

She'd never had a man to turn to in the night, never had someone she could depend on to keep her safe. She squeezed, just a little, and he moaned, found her mouth in the dark, his breath musky with sleep. She didn't release him, stroking him to fullness as he unbuttoned her top, pushed down her pants.

The rustle of cellophane filled the room and he pushed her away, was over her, inside her, rocking her, filling her, fulfilling her.

She ran her fingers down his back to curve over his ass, holding him to her, arching toward him, her mouth hungry beneath his. He scooped her hair back with one hand, lifted her hips with the other and they found a rhythm that pleased them

175

both. She didn't want it to end, didn't want the pleasure, the connection to end, but with one shift of his hips, she tumbled over the edge and dragged him with her.

They lay together afterwards. Tangled together, they fell asleep.

Hours later, Isabella woke to find herself alone, sheets pulled over her naked body. Sunlight dappled the bed, filtered through the leaves of the trees and the trailer's dirty windows. Outside, birds competed for the loudest cry. She must have been tired to sleep through that. She heard movement in the kitchen and, finding her pajamas and shoes, she made her way down the hall.

Alex crouched in front of the refrigerator in his boxers and T-shirt, scrubbing. The sour scent filled the air, along with the tinny sound of the little radio on the counter, talking about the shuttle launch.

"Cell phone doesn't work out here," he said without looking up. "I'm surprised that thing does. I cleaned the bathroom too. You can take a bath if you want."

She pushed her hair out of her face and scanned the trailer, which didn't improve in daylight. It did smell better, though, the combination of cleaning solution and coffee making it almost homey. "How long have you been up?" *How long are we staying here*, she wanted to ask.

"Couple of hours."

"What time is it?"

He pushed to his feet to rinse off the rag in the sink. "Just after noon."

She jolted. "So late?"

"We got in about three, so, yeah. Don't worry. You needed

the sleep."

Still, she'd lost all that time, time they could have been looking for her son. She bit back the words. There was nothing to be done about it, and to harp on it would seem petty.

"You made coffee," she said instead, reaching across the trailer for the small pot.

"Mug there is clean. There are Nutri-Grain bars in one of those bags there. If you want, I can heat up some chili or something."

"No, it's okay." She lifted the steaming mug to her mouth and wondering where Domestic Alex had come from. The coffee smelled wonderful, and she wasn't ordinarily a coffee drinker.

For a moment the trailer was silent except for the softly accented female voice on the radio, one of the astronauts from the shuttle flight.

"So what's the plan?" she asked.

He sat back on his heels. "You shower, we drive somewhere to get a signal, call my team, let them know we're okay, see what they've found out."

"Okay. We have a plan." She set the mug on the table behind her, feeling much lighter.

When he pushed himself to a standing position, suddenly the trailer seemed a lot smaller. Something like fondness shone in his eyes. He stroked her hair back, trailing his fingers along her jaw. Her nerves jumped in response.

"Those pajamas make me crazy," he murmured and covered her mouth with his.

She bowed into him, cupping the back of his head, savoring his familiar taste, memories of last night flooding her, arousing her.

"You smell like bleach."

"Sorry." He snatched his hands back.

She grabbed them, brought them to her face and sniffed them. "I don't mind."

He kissed her again, his mouth demanding. He lifted her, carrying her down the hall. She wrapped her legs around him and clung even as he bounced her off a corner, a wall, and finally onto the bed, following her down. He rose up just enough to unbutton her top, his breathing hot and fast, and he flashed a grin at her.

Alex. Grinned. At her.

Her heart tumbled all over itself.

He kissed the hollow of her throat, eased his way down, worshipfully, as if each kiss gave him the same pleasure it gave her.

Alex could smell himself on her skin as he kissed her collarbone, the swell of her breast, before he dragged his tongue around her nipple ad continued down her flat belly. He nipped her navel before ascending again, capturing her other nipple between his lips, tugging till she gasped in pleasure.

Sliding his fingers down the front of her pants, he found her hot and slick. His own desire had been barely banked since she'd turned to him in the dark last night. He hadn't been able to stop thinking about it since he woke, the way she'd reached for him, the way they'd come together so easily, moved together so easily, found pleasure.

It wasn't supposed to be like that, especially not with her. That it had been, well, he wanted to feel it again. And again. When she'd walked out this morning in those damn pajamas—

She slid her palm down his belly and into his shorts, circling him, as eager as he was, and he was naked, then sheathed, then inside her and she was moving into him, her body straining, glistening, glowing in the midday light.

He dropped over her, pushed her hair back and kissed her deeply while she wound her arms around his neck, slick with sweat, with effort, with his impending orgasm.

Breaking the kiss, he looked into her eyes as he vaulted over the edge, felt her holding on to him, unsure if she followed.

"Christ, Bella," he managed, dropping to his side next to her. "I don't usually have such a hair trigger."

Without a word, she turned onto her side, sliding her hand across his shoulder to his chest, tucking her head between his neck and shoulder. He stroked her side, over her hip, watched her skin jump, sending him the signal he was looking for. She hadn't come with him.

He dealt with the condom, then nestled her closer to him, teased her thighs apart as he stroked her open. She reacted like an electric shock had gone through her, but he wasn't going to make it that easy for her. He dragged his touch down to her opening, teasing her, caressing until she tensed, then retreating.

"You have kind of a hair trigger yourself," he murmured, dipping his fingers into her, feeling her squeeze around him.

He was getting hard again. Damn, he'd made love to her three times in the past twenty-four hours. Only teenagers were supposed to be able to recover so fast, right? But he knew the reason, if he cared to admit it.

"Bella."

He kissed her soft mouth, his touch playing between her smooth thighs, stringing her tight as a bow, and then he was ready, over her, in her, and she was crying out, clinging to him, bowing beneath him.

He tucked his head into the curve of her throat and rode out her orgasm, knowing he wouldn't follow.

He didn't need to.

She smiled up at him, a lopsided smile, like she didn't have control of her muscles. The idea, the smile, made him feel like king of the world.

Christ, he was treading thin ice, here, putting his expectations on her. Just like he'd done with Rebecca.

She reached up to bring his head down for a kiss, but he broke away.

"Better get cleaned up so we can find a signal."

The confusion couldn't have been clearer on her face. Yes, he was a bastard. Knowing that, he still pushed off the bed away from her.

Chapter Thirteen

The ease they'd shared was gone. Isabella sat as far across the truck as she could as they drove out of the forest in search of a cell signal. Alex's rare grin was again missing, and she had to wonder if it was because they were trying to contact the real world. He seemed to prefer the isolation of the trailer.

He'd barely spoken since he rolled off the bed and she'd headed for the clean shower. When they got back in the truck, he'd given her the assignment to watch the bars on his phone, to let him know when they got a signal. At least she had something to do to make her feel productive. And to keep her mind off his sudden desire to put distance between them.

He had the truck radio on, a country-western station. She let the music wash past her, too sad at the emptiness of her lost connection to Alex and her helplessness in finding her son to listen to someone else's heartbreak.

She perked up when the news came on. The shuttle launch again.

"Why are they making such a big deal about this?" she asked, forgetting for a minute he'd ignored her since they'd made love.

"First Muslim woman on a shuttle. She moved to the US to join the program, left her family behind. A big decision for her."

"Hector's fascinated with rockets. All the noise, I guess.

And the idea of seeing stars up close."

"If we find him in time, we'll take him to see the launch."

She blinked in surprise. Had he really offered to see her, to see her son, after this was over? Was he talking about a future? His jaw clenched, as if he hadn't meant to say the kind words aloud, as if he hadn't meant to talk about a time after they found Hector, a time when she wouldn't need him anymore.

The future she was holding her breath trying to reach.

"He'll love that."

She turned away when he nodded once, brusquely. She studied the scenery out her window, trees giving way to brush and marsh, large birds wandering the side of the road, picking their way through high grass, searching for food, not spooked by the rumbling of the truck's engine. Strange, since she didn't see any other cars along this stretch of road. Where was everyone?

They found a signal about the time they found a gas station. Alex traded her a pair of twenties for the phone.

"You go in and pay. I'll pump it when I get done here." He indicated the phone.

"I know how to pump gas," she protested, but he was already moving away, pressing his free hand over his opposite ear as he spoke into the phone. She followed his movement with her gaze, wishing she knew who he was talking to, what he was telling them. Who did he trust with their whereabouts? After last night, she wasn't sure who she trusted, even Alex's friend Danes. She didn't think Alex had told him where they were staying, but he'd turned up at their hotel. Yes, he'd gotten them out of danger, but she had to wonder why he'd been there.

Alex was still on the phone when she was done pumping gas, so she went inside the tiny gas station to retrieve his change. The headlines announced news on the shuttle launch.

182

Intrigued, Isabella picked it up, then gathered some snacks. She'd forgotten how ready treats were in the United States, there for mere cents.

So easy, she'd weigh a ton if she didn't cut back.

She wondered if Alex would mind if she put on some weight. She wondered what he'd do if she ended up pregnant with his child.

That thought came out of nowhere, kicking her in the sternum. When had she started thinking about after she got Hector back? That had been her goal for so long, she'd been afraid to consider what would come next.

She knew better than to expect Alex would be part of her future. He was more likely to bolt once she had Hector safe and sound. For all that he enjoyed her body, she didn't get the idea that he liked her very much.

If he didn't bolt, did she want a man in her life who had a job that put his life at risk? She needed security for her and her child. Alex was not that man.

It didn't matter. After this was over, he would no longer be in her life. He didn't love her. She didn't love him. She only needed him. She would be wise not to confuse the two.

She stepped out of the station as he flipped the phone closed and made his way back to the truck. She tossed him a candy bar, which he caught one-handed against his chest.

"Anything?" she asked.

He motioned with his head for her to get in the cab. "I was talking to my captain, who's been in touch with the DEA. They found Pablo in Texas. No sign he has Hector. They have him in custody in San Antonio."

"And Carmen?"

He shook his head. "Nothing yet."

183

"No word on Santiago."

"Not yet." He opened the bottle of Coke she'd passed over. "I'm sorry."

"How long before we can start looking again?"

He tossed the bottle cap on the dashboard and sighed. "Bella, the problem is, we don't know where to look."

"I should have let those men at the hotel take me," she said, bitter regret choking her words. They would have taken her to Santiago, and though she'd be back in the life she'd escaped, she would be with her son.

"What makes you think they would have taken you to your son? Saldana separated you in the first place. I doubt he's looking to reunite you. You wouldn't do Hector any good dead."

She pushed her hair from her face as her stomach tightened. Santiago would have punished her somehow, she knew. "You don't know they were going to kill me."

Alex snorted. "I'm thinking they weren't there to court you."

She couldn't let go of the what-if. "But you could have followed and rescued me, and we could have found Hector and this would all be over."

He chuckled without humor. "Amazing, the faith you have in me."

"You wouldn't have let him get away with it. Even if he'd killed me, you would have found my son and made sure he was safe."

He didn't say anything, just took a long drink of his Coke. "I'm going to protect you. That's my first job. All right?"

"I want Hector to be your priority."

"I can't do that."

"Alex, listen to me." She turned in her seat and rested her hand on his arm. "He's just a baby. He needs your protection
184

more than I do. If anything happens to me—"

The muscle in his jaw jumped but he kept his eyes ahead. "Nothing's going to happen to you."

"I know. I trust you to keep me safe." How could she think otherwise, after all he'd pulled her through, even after he had the opportunity to walk away back in Honduras? But those men last night had had guns. Santiago had sent men after her to Jorge's club. People had died. There were no guarantees here. "But if something does, I do not want Hector to go with Santiago or any of his family."

Alex shifted his weight, breaking away from her touch.

"It's not that I want you to take him," she said quickly. "Though I'm sure someday you'll be a good dad and all that. I'd just never ask that of you after you've done so much for me. But I want you to see that he'll get to someone who will love him."

"Your parents?" he asked, glancing sharply at her.

Those words caused more pain than she expected. They brought back images of another lifetime, one she never should have left behind. Only if she'd followed that path, she wouldn't have Hector now and she wouldn't give him up for anything. She glanced at the newspaper in her lap. "No, they won't—I mean, they'd love him, but they're not young. And—"

"They don't know about him," he finished for her.

She looked up at him. "No, I haven't told them."

"I wouldn't know what to do with a little kid, providing the authorities let me do anything at all. But it doesn't matter, because nothing is going to happen to you, all right?" He glanced over, his eyebrows drawn together, intense, as if he could drill that belief into her head. "You and Hector will be safe, this will be over, we'll all go to Disney World."

She stopped the thrill that ran through her. Wasn't that what everyone said when they achieved a goal? "I'm going to Disney World?" She would not take it personally.

He turned on the ignition, and the voice on the radio startled them both. Alex reached over and snapped it off. "Remind me. How long has he been missing?"

"Four months."

He blew a breath through his nose, almost a surrender, she thought. "We're going to find him, Bella. I promise you."

What did that cost him, to promise her something he had no way of guaranteeing? She didn't know how to tell him she appreciated it, either.

"There's a diner. Let's eat there," she said instead, pointing to the low-roofed restaurant that must have been built before she was born. Her growling stomach reminded her she hadn't eaten before he took her back to bed.

He grimaced. "We have food at the trailer."

She wanted to bounce in her seat in frustration, like Hector would. She could smell the fries and her mouth was watering. "But it's right here, and I haven't eaten at a diner in forever."

"We don't know how long we have to make our money last," he reminded her. "Besides, when I talked to Lionel, he wanted me to check on some traps. I want to do it before it gets dark."

She made a face. "He poaches?"

"Yeah, probably, but he's doing us a big favor. Do you want to turn him in?"

"If I was going to turn him in, it would be for the condition of that cabin," she muttered, glancing down at the newspaper and trying to convince her mouth canned chili was something to look forward to.

They rode back to the trailer in silence. Isabella found she couldn't read in the truck that bounced along the unpaved roads, so she tucked it beneath her and ate a candy bar, aware of Alex's disapproval.

"I'll make lunch, then go check the traps," he said when he parked. "You can eat your junk and read while I'm out."

"I'm feeling pretty worthless," she murmured. "I can make lunch. All I have to do is open a couple of cans, right?"

"Sure."

Once they entered the cabin, though, they were silent again as she found the cans and pots and rinsed them out. She couldn't stop thinking about the morning, how he'd made love to her, then turned away so abruptly. Something had changed.

Something that kept him quiet as he made his way down the narrow hall to the bedroom.

Lunch was ready quickly. They ate standing up since the table was still crowded with their supplies from Walmart. She opened a can of peaches too and savored the sweetness of the fruit packed in syrup. She glanced over to see him looking at her oddly.

He set his paper plate on the counter, dusted off his hands and opened the door. "I'm going to go check those traps."

"Be careful. Alligators."

He nodded. "And snakes. I've got my gun." He patted his hip, under his shirt. "You stay inside."

Had he been armed when they stopped for gas? Maybe that was why he hadn't wanted to stop for food. Surely he didn't think they were in danger out here.

She washed up in the kitchen, feeling very domestic. She'd never had a home of her own, with responsibilities. That had been her mother's life, the life she'd been escaping. But now, for some reason, she found it satisfying. When she was done, she folded the washcloth over the sink, then took the paper and one of her novels, along with the remainder of her Diet Coke, and went back to the bedroom, the only place to sit in the cabin.

She hadn't realized she'd drifted off while reading until she woke when gravel crunched beneath tires on the road in front of the cabin. She didn't think Alex had taken the truck.

Her heart pounded at the thought of intruders. She had seen a few guns just inside the screened porch, but even if they were loaded, she didn't know how to use them. Would she be able to get to them in time, and without being seen?

She eased to the window and pushed aside the curtain a mere centimeter. Relief exploded in her. Lionel Danes. Thank God. But what was he doing out here? Maybe he had news and wasn't able to reach them by phone. Excited by the possibility, she tucked her feet in her shoes and hurried to the door, pushing the screen open in welcome.

"Mr. Danes," she greeted, heart pounding in anticipation. Maybe he'd found something to lead them to Hector. Maybe he'd found Hector already. "Alex isn't here—he went to go check your traps."

The old man nodded as if it was what he expected. "He can meet us. But we need to go back to the city."

As he approached, every nerve went on alert. His face was grim, not bearing the news she'd hoped. He wanted her to go without Alex. She didn't want to leave him behind. She didn't want to be alone with this man. "Go back? Why? I thought it was too dangerous."

"They found out where you are." He came forward in two strides and took her arm. "They traced Alex's phone call."

Pulse tripping, she looked down at his grip, which squeezed her arm tighter than necessary. She tried to pull free, to go back in the cabin. She didn't want him to see her panic, and this close, he wouldn't miss it. Maybe once inside, she could act casual and stall him until Alex returned. "I'll just get my things."

Danes shook his head, jaw set stubbornly. "No time. No telling how far they are behind me."

"Alex—"

"He can take care of himself."

"He won't know where I've gone."

"We'll call him."

"His phone doesn't work out here. Please, just let me leave him a note and get my purse."

"No time," Danes repeated and tugged her toward the truck.

She looked past him down the empty road, twisted, her arm still captive in his big rough hand, to look behind her. Her stomach clenched. No sign of Alex. Danes was still pulling her, and she dug in the heels of her Keds and tried to tug free.

"I want to wait for Alex," she said.

"Alex would want me to get you out of here."

That was true, if there was danger. She took a couple more steps toward the truck, then stopped. "He'll be worried when he sees I didn't take anything."

"Girly, do you give him this much trouble?" Danes asked, turning in frustration.

"Yes."

With a growl, he dipped his shoulder and tucked it into her belly, swinging her over his shoulder. The abrupt movement knocked her breath out of her so she couldn't scream before he tossed her in the passenger side of the truck.

Once she was in, she fought for breath and screamed her

lungs out, scrambling for the window to roll it down. Surely Alex would hear her. Surely Alex would come.

Danes lunged through the driver's side door and tackled her, clubbing her hard on the side of the head so she saw spots and lost her breath. Then he hit her again and she lost everything else.

Alex came back to the cabin hot, sweaty and frustrated. He didn't know what the hell kind of traps Danes had been talking about because he'd followed the old man's directions exactly and hadn't found traps or animals. He had killed a big-ass snake and brought it back to show Isabella. Maybe that was a bad idea, maybe the carcass would freak her out, but he thought it was cool. He'd tease her a bit and tell her it was dinner. He'd love to see her face when she thought she'd have to eat it.

Maybe he'd take her back to that diner, tell her he had to check in again. She'd seemed so danged wistful.

But first, he needed a shower. He walked over to his truck to drape the snake over the tailgate, and that's when he saw the stirred-up gravel.

Someone else had been here.

He whipped his head up. "Bella," he shouted, his voice echoing back through the wilderness. "Bella?" He ran to the cabin, saw the door between the cabin and the screened patio open and her purse on the table. "Bella!" The trailer sounded hollow, empty. Had a neighbor come upon them, or had someone else found them? He knew Saldana had resources, but damn.

He pushed the thought out of his head. She could be looking for him, though he could hardly see her picking her way through the wilderness, unless she wanted him very, very badly. His heart jumped into his throat and he circled around. Which way could she have gone?

No, she wouldn't have gone. She was too skittish about the alligators and snakes. Someone had been here. Someone had taken her. But who?

Chapter Fourteen

Alex sped down the dirt road with his arm stretched in front of him as he held the phone, glancing from the road to the phone, looking at the bars.

He'd gone around the cabin but hadn't seen any sign that Isabella had walked into the wilderness. She had to have gone in the vehicle. With dread grabbing hold, he'd tracked the vehicle onto the paved road, and north, but from there, he couldn't tell where they'd gone. His chest tightened with fear, but he pushed it away. This was his job. He couldn't think about Isabella and whatever feelings he had for her. He couldn't think about how scared she would be. He had to follow the clues to learn who had her, where they'd taken her and how he'd find her. He wished he knew how much of a head start they had.

No bars yet. Shit. Shit, shit, shit. He pounded his fist against the steering wheel, looked across the cab at her purse, beside the rest of her things that he'd flung into the truck. She'd left the cabin without them, so she must have gone out to meet whoever had come. He hadn't seen any sign of struggle inside.

Had it been Saldana's men? Someone had to know how to secure her cooperation. Whoever it was had more than likely used Hector.

How many people knew about her searching for her son? Too many, and that was his fault. He should have kept that information quiet, should have known it could be used against her. He just hadn't thought someone would come out to the Everglades to find her.

Finally two bars. He dialed with his left thumb, swerving a little on the two-lane road. He brought the phone to his ear and as soon as Julian answered, he barked, "Where's Isabella?"

Nausea rose up in Isabella as Lionel Danes barreled over the bumpy road. She couldn't tell if her stomach rebelled because of the road, or the blow to her head, or the terror that lumped the chili in her stomach. Alex had trusted this man to keep them safe, and he'd betrayed them.

"Are you working for Santiago?" she managed.

He glanced over with a jerk of his head, as if surprised she was conscious. He hadn't bound her, her hands were free. She was only restricted by the seat belt. What she would do about it, at this speed, she didn't know.

Alex would know what to do. She needed to think like Alex. He would try to get as much information as he could, no doubt. So she swallowed her nerves and pressed.

"Is Santiago paying you?"

"There's a price on your head."

Her skin iced. "Dead or alive?"

He blew out a harsh breath, his attention back on the road. "More alive than dead. But I think that's because it's his preference to punish you."

"Does he have my son?" Because if she had that to look forward to, she could calm down. Then it wouldn't matter so much if Alex couldn't find her. At least she'd have her child.

Danes didn't answer.

"Do you even know?"

No answer.

His phone rang and Isabella tensed, but he didn't react. He glanced at the display, then at her, before answering it.

"Who knew we were out here?"

She could hear Alex's voice through the phone. Danes must have the volume turned up high. Relief washed through her. "Alex!"

Hesitation on his end, a roll of the eyes from Danes, then, "You?" Disbelief from Alex. Betrayal? She could hear it even through the phone's tiny speaker. "You sent me out on those traps so you could come get her?"

The older man sighed. "I didn't want to fight you." He almost sounded sorry.

"You didn't have to fight her?"

"Just a little tap to the head." Danes looked over at her and grinned, thin lips stretching. "She's nice and feisty now."

"Where are you taking her?"

"You don't want to follow, son, believe me. Let it go."

"You know I can't do that."

"I warned you not to get involved."

She couldn't hear what Alex said next because his phone crackled. Her initial relief at hearing his voice returned to panic. He was still too far away. "We're in an SUV, Alex," she shouted toward the phone, hoping he could hear her. "A big blue one, a Chevy—"

Lionel backhanded her, sending her head bumping off the passenger window. She cried out and heard Alex swear as Lionel righted the vehicle on the road. Liquid gushed into her mouth, a coppery taste, and her ears rang as she tried to focus on the conversation.

"I'm just a delivery guy, son."

"Delivering her to Santiago?"

Danes was silent.

"He's going to kill her."

The connection was clear now, because Isabella could hear the frustration in Alex's voice.

"Not sure he will," Danes lied, though to appease her or Alex, Isabella wasn't sure. "Make her suffer, most certainly. But you know women like this, my boy. She deserves what she gets, no matter how tasty she is."

Her skin crawled when the old man reached across the cab to caress the cheek he'd just hit.

"Lionel, don't do this."

Danes turned his focus back to the phone. "You're mistaking lust for affection, Alex."

"She's a mother looking for her kid. He's just a little guy. What chance is he going to have without her?"

The old man's expression in the dashboard light tightened. "With the price on her head, what chance will I have?"

Isabella understood, then. He was in debt to Santiago in some way and she was the payment. She was nothing more than currency. He must have crossed a line with Santiago. He must really believe turning her over would get him off.

"It's a done deal, Alex," Danes continued. "Walk away."

"I can't do that."

"Look, son, I'm sure she's a nice piece of ass, but you know as well as I do, they're a dime a dozen. Walk. Away."

"No, sir. I'm coming after her." Alex hung up.

Isabella's heart tripped over his words. He was coming after her.

How, she had no idea.

Several miles passed before she dared speak again. Her cheek still stung from his last blow. But anger and resentment bubbled forth, and she decided to risk speaking out.

"He trusted you," she said, low.

He glanced at her in surprise, as if he'd forgotten she was there. "What?"

She gained confidence, straightening in her seat as she turned to him. "He came to you because he trusted you."

"I didn't hurt him. I didn't want to hurt him." The old man was on the defensive. Did he really think he'd done nothing wrong?

"You betrayed his trust. To Alex, that's the same thing."

He whipped around on her, and the truck swerved in the lane. "What do you know about Alex? For that matter, what do you know about trust?"

"I trust Alex," she said, lifting her chin. "He said he'd come after me and he means it."

"I'm a Ranger, like him. He won't choose a woman over a fellow Ranger."

The words silenced her for a minute. Maybe he was right. But no, the Alex she knew protected those who couldn't protect themselves. The choice wouldn't be easy, but he would choose her.

Maybe he would hate her afterward for making him choose.

She couldn't care. She had to stay alive, had to get away, had to stick with Alex until she found her son. That was more important than anything else.

Isabella could see the lights of a city glowing ahead. Which city, she didn't know, but they were approaching civilization.

And anonymity. The realization chilled her.

Danes would ditch the SUV, or it would blend in with others, and he'd put her back in Santiago's custody. Her only hope was that Hector would be there too and that she would survive Santiago's wrath to raise her son.

Before they reached the outskirts of the city, Danes turned right, onto a long narrow stretch of road. She felt the car hesitate, as if he'd eased off the accelerator, as if he was having second thoughts. She wouldn't have another chance.

"Santiago will kill me," she murmured, hoping she could appeal to his human nature but hearing the hopelessness in her own voice. Of course, if he had a conscience, would he be doing this? "Can you live with that?"

"I've lived with worse."

She swallowed the tears she'd held back for days. "All I want is to raise my son. Please, you have to turn back."

He cast her a disgusted look. "Those tears may work on Shepard, but they won't work on me."

Just the mention of Alex's name was another kick in the gut. She wouldn't see him again. Would he find Hector for her and keep him safe? Or would he forget about her? No, he was too honorable. He would get to her son because he was a protector. He would punish himself for not protecting her.

She dropped her concern for Alex the moment Danes rounded a hangar and she saw two black SUVs parked at odd angles around a small plane, headlights blazing through the dusk. Even with the six men in silhouette in front of them, she recognized the stocky shape of Santiago Saldana.

Alex snatched up the phone the minute it rang. Thanks to

Julian tracing Danes's GPS, they were tracking the man and Isabella, who had started out about forty-five minutes before him. With his foot to the floorboard, Alex had been able to make up most of that time before he contacted Danes and alerted the older man.

"Where are they?"

"A private airfield west of Miami. You should be close," Julian said. "We're at the base now, getting a chopper out. Don't go in on your own."

Alex snapped his teeth together. Going in alone was against everything he'd been trained to do, but one thought was foremost in his mind. "He has Isabella."

"You don't know what you're walking into. Wait for us. We'll be there in half an hour."

"That's too late."

"Saldana won't be there."

Julian thought that was what worried him? Of course he did. What else did Alex care about? Julian didn't know what Saldana had done to Isabella. He only knew Saldana was the mission objective.

"He'll get away."

"Better he get away than you get dead. We're at the helo now. Wait."

Alex folded the phone and tossed it on the seat beside him before accelerating. The hell he would.

Good thing Danes had such a firm grip on Isabella's arm, because her knees could barely hold her when he dragged her from the truck to come face to face with her nightmare. She was shaking all over, unable to hide her weakness. Had she learned nothing from Alex? With that thought in the forefront of her brain, she forced her chin up as Santiago took three deliberate steps toward her.

Only a few months had passed since she'd seen him, but he'd lost weight, and gravity dragged at the loose skin of his cheeks and jaw. His dark eyes appeared sunken, the skin around them baggy and lined. Still, his body was powerful, broad shouldered, stocky, his hands wide and strong and capable of inflicting pain at the slightest frustration.

She swallowed hard and did her best not to flinch from his gaze. "I want to see Hector."

"I do not care what you want. You have caused me too much trouble, wasted too much of my time looking for you."

"I didn't ask you to look for me."

He took another step. His expression was relaxed but his eyes were hard, flat. She knew that look and cowered against Danes despite herself. He didn't move away or shake her off, oddly, though he stood stiff when Santiago flicked his gaze to the bigger man then back to her.

"You belong to me."

The last of her courage was buried deep, but she found it and dragged it up. "Not anymore."

He swung in an arc toward her but she didn't duck, taking the blow full on the cheek. Her skin split and she staggered into the front fender of Danes's truck, realizing he wasn't holding on to her anymore. The heat of the engine beneath the metal seared her palms, but she didn't have the energy to push away for a moment.

She was at Santiago's mercy. From experience she knew that he had none.

The squeal of tires behind her made her heart jolt, turned Santiago's attention away. She knew the sound of that engine.

God help her, Alex had come. She shoved her hair out of her face, looked toward him, past Santiago. Her heart dropped, her hope with it.

He was alone, against seven men.

But Alex didn't hesitate. He shoved open the truck door and ducked behind it, his pistol in front of him, trained on one man.

Beside her, Santiago laughed and moved in front of her, toward Alex. "The shining knight has arrived, Isabella," he said, his voice booming. "Do you remember what I did to your last shining knight?"

She would never forget watching Eric die, screaming, then whispering her name. What had happened afterward, to her, hadn't been as horrible. She could not bear living it again. She couldn't let Alex die that way, but was powerless. "There's nothing between us," she lied, desperate, knowing Alex heard, hoping her words didn't hurt. But it was the only way she could think to save his life.

He'd come for her. Had risked his life. The reality of the danger they were in threatened to choke her. Meeting Saldana had been more acceptable, less frightening, when only her life was at stake. Her gaze riveted on Alex, his lean face illuminated by the headlights, the muscle in his arms corded as he held the gun straight in front of him. A real hero. But he was all by himself.

"Send her over here." Alex didn't shout the words, but they carried a level of command she'd never heard him use.

Santiago shook his head slowly. "You are brave but foolish." He looked back at Isabella with a bemused expression. "What is it about you that makes men willing to die for you?" Turning toward Alex, he reached inside his jacket.

The headlights glinted off metal as Santiago drew his gun.

"Alex!" she screamed in warning, frozen as she watched Santiago extend the weapon in slow motion.

"Get down," Alex shouted at the same time.

Her muscles tightened, unable to obey his command until the first shot rang out over the tarmac, then her body loosened and she dropped to the asphalt, covering her head with her arms as gunfire erupted, striking the metal of the vehicles, eliciting shouts of pain, drawing the scent of blood.

Afterward, she would count less than ten shots, but an eternity passed before she could lift her head. Lionel Danes lay at her feet, vacant eyes staring at the darkening sky. Santiago stood at an odd angle, favoring one side, and blood dripped down one arm, pooling on the ground.

Beside his truck, Alex lay on his back, one leg bent. Completely still.

Chapter Fifteen

She screamed his name and scrambled toward him, only to be snatched back by the hair, stumbling, scraping her forearm on the asphalt. Despite the pain, like needles prickling her scalp, and the gravel tearing at her skin, she clawed the ground to get away, to get to Alex. Her throat burned with unshed tears, with an agony no amount of screaming could alleviate. He couldn't be dead. He couldn't. Not because of her. But if he was alive, he would be moving. He would be trying to get to her.

The scene was a nightmare. She couldn't reach him. Her vision telescoped and suddenly her breath was forced from her lungs as one of the other men lifted her over his shoulder, carrying her away, away from Alex.

He hadn't moved. Not a muscle.

She kicked, twisted, screamed, but was held firm and dumped in the SUV. As soon as the man released her, she bounced out of her seat, heading for the door, only to be met by a fist to the temple.

And blackness.

Alex fought for breath as he stared at the sky and heard the plane's engines start. Damn it, damn it, Isabella was on that plane and he couldn't move, couldn't go after her. The stars blurred, darkened, came back into focus, but only silence now. The plane was gone.

Isabella was gone. His gut churned with pain and despair. He'd failed her. She was back in the hands of the monster.

The next thing he knew, Julian was over him, cursing him, and ripping the bullet proof vest from him. Alex couldn't pick out his words because, well, Alex was trying to draw air into his lungs without pain. What had they shot him with, a cannon? His chest felt like it had caved in.

Then he realized Julian was cursing him in Spanish. Too much effort to listen, to translate. Instead, he grabbed his friend's arm and forced his attention. "Saldana was here. He took Isabella."

"We've got satellite tracking him," Julian said grimly. "I told you not to engage."

"He took Isabella," Alex repeated, each syllable a struggle.

"Yeah, well, you didn't save her now, did you?"

Alex let his head fall back to the asphalt, released Julian's shirt. "He's going to kill her." After he made her suffer for leaving him.

"We've got eyes on him, buddy. We know where he's going."

Alex shoved himself up on one elbow, but the movement made him dizzy as hell, and nauseated. His head throbbed like a son of a bitch. Still. "I've got to get to her."

"You've got to get to the hospital for some x-rays," Julian retorted. "Looks like you hit your head pretty good. Might need some stitches. There isn't a plan in place yet, anyway."

Alex ground his teeth. "The longer she's with him, the more danger she's in."

"It won't be long," Julian insisted. "You just need to get patched up. We'll get her back."

"You keep an eye on her." He scanned the area, what he

could see with his telescoping vision. Great. A concussion. Just what he needed. "I got Danes and some of Saldana's men. They still down?"

Julian glanced behind him. "I don't see any bodies. Lots of blood, though."

"Didn't get Saldana—scared I'd hit Bella. Stupid."

"Not stupid. You can't risk a hostage."

"Not a hostage."

She wasn't—she was the woman he'd sworn to protect, a woman who trusted him to keep her safe. He'd failed her.

"The SUVs? There were two. Expeditions, I think." He strained to see past Julian's shoulder across the dark tarmac.

"Gone."

He closed his eyes again. "Maybe surveillance footage—"

"We got it covered, Shep. We'll take care of it."

"Don't let him hurt her," Alex said and passed out.

Alex sat on the narrow cot in the emergency room and watched for the nurse he'd sent to get him a shirt. Bruised ribs, they said. Could have been worse. Thank God he kept the vest behind the seat of his truck, and had taken time to put it on. Also, a minor concussion, and eight stitches in his scalp. Still, the amount of blood on his shirt made it look like he'd been butchered.

Julian was coming to pick him up now. Why he couldn't have attended to Alex in the field, Alex didn't know. It wasn't like he'd never gotten stitches without anesthetic, or continued on a mission with a concussion. The rest of the team probably wanted him out of the way while they made their plan, the bastards. Julian had better be here before the nurse returned—or Alex would walk back to DEA headquarters, find out what they'd learned from satellite and cell phones. He didn't know if they were still tracking Bella or if they'd found Saldana. Goddamn, he hated being helpless.

He had to force himself not to think about what she was enduring, only what he could control.

Which wasn't a hell of a lot.

The nurse returned with a shirt. Her lips pressed together matter-of-factly as he grimaced. He pushed her hands away to button it himself.

"You have my phone?" he asked.

"Your ride will be here soon enough," she said shortly.

"I want to call my dad." Tell him he'd killed his friend. Get absolution. Hear his voice.

The woman's eyes softened marginally. "Yeah. I can get you your phone. I'll be right back."

For the first time he hoped Julian wouldn't come just yet. He needed to talk to his father with the privacy of a confessional.

The nurse returned with his personal effects. He dug out his phone, and holding it reassured him. He hadn't realized how out of touch he'd felt. He dialed with shaking fingers. "Dad."

"Hello, son," his foster father replied in his deep, calm voice.

"Dad, I—" He swallowed hard, shaking all over now. "I just killed Lionel Danes."

He heard his dad's intake of breath, could sense him controlling his questions, knowing as a former Ranger himself what he could and couldn't ask.

"What happened?"

That question left it open to Alex to decide what to share.

"It's my fault," Alex said. "I went to him. I needed his help here and he got us out of town and gave us a place to stay, and then—he took the woman I'm trying to protect."

"Took her?"

Alex swallowed against the burning in his throat. "Kidnapped her. I thought she was safe alone, he came and got her. He said she had a price on her head. He was holding a gun to her—" He broke off.

"You were assigned to keep this woman safe." His father's voice was calm, reasonable, as Alex had hoped it would be. Had feared it wouldn't be.

"No. I was assigned to let her lead us back to the bad guy."

"Ah." The single syllable held a world of meaning.

"It's not like that." Damn, he never lied to his foster father. Not anymore. Usually his father could see through it. Alex had to hope the phone gave them enough distance. "She's young, she's looking for her child. He's only three years old. A kid that young needs his mother, right?"

"He does." His father dragged out the last word leadingly.

"I made a mistake." Alex rubbed a hand down his face as if he could erase that fact. "More than one. Lionel Danes is dead because of it. She's gone, taken by the man Lionel gave her to. Because I worried more about the woman than the job."

"Alex, you're a good soldier. Lionel Danes was a man who always had his own best interests at heart."

Alex resisted the pull of those words, the hope that they were true. "He was a Ranger."

"You know yourself not all Rangers are saints."

He did know. "But if I hadn't killed him, he could link us to Saldana, to the kid."

"He still could. You just have to work backwards. If he was

in that deep, he would have killed you to get what he wanted, Alex."

"I know." He'd heard it in the old man's voice earlier tonight. "I know."

"You did what you had to do, Alex. You've done it before. Odds are you'll have to do it again."

His father was right. Hell, he may have to do it before this was over.

"Call me when you can," his father said with a sigh when Alex didn't say anything. "I love you, son."

"I love you too, Dad." He flipped the phone closed just as Julian walked back. The grim look on the younger man's face made Alex's stomach twist. "What happened?"

"We lost Saldana."

Alex's stomach dropped, and he jumped to his feet, ignoring his swimming head. "Isabella?"

"We don't know."

"Where did you lose track?" He grabbed up the plastic bag with his belongings and started for the exit, staggering just a bit on unsteady legs.

Julian fell into step. "Near Jacksonville."

But at least not heading back to Honduras. How long had it taken the DEA to find Saldana the first time? Years? Isabella didn't have that long.

"Have they traced the SUVs? What about the plane? It's not like there are a lot of places they could land—did you get the flight plan?"

"Yeah, we have it, and we have a team on its way to the airstrip, but Saldana's avoided authorities for a long damn time. You don't think he's playing by the rules now, do you?"

Alex whirled on his friend, who steadied him when he

swayed. "We've got to start somewhere, got to find her."

Jesus. What was she going through right now? Because if Saldana touched her, Alex would tear him apart. She'd been through enough.

He slammed his fist on the gurney. "How could you lose her? Do you know what he'll do to her?"

Julian shook his head. "I'm sorry, Shep."

"I shouldn't have left her alone. I trusted Danes, and I left her alone while I did him a favor. I killed her."

Julian rested his hand on Alex's shoulder. "We'll get to her in time."

Alex shook his head. "It's already too late."

Isabella woke on a rolling bed, the scent of fish—no, the scent of the ocean—surrounding her. She took a quick inventory. Her head and her stomach ached from where Santiago had hit her once she was in his custody, but she was dressed and hadn't been raped.

Thank God.

But Alex was dead, and that was the worst pain of all.

Without opening her eyes, she tried to measure the room, to discover if anyone was here with her. She listened for the sound of breathing, anything that would give her a clue. But she heard nothing but the lapping of waves against the hull. A boat, then, but no motor. No other sounds surrounded the boat, no voices, no other boats. They had to be in open water. How would anyone find her now?

Slowly she opened her eyes. The room was clean, bright enough to hurt her eyes, gleaming wood and brass. A yacht.

She sat up abruptly. Hector could be here. If Santiago was leaving the country, he would certainly bring his son.

The fact that she wasn't bound struck her and reaffirmed her fear that they were out on the ocean. Nowhere to run.

She was his prisoner again.

She rolled off the bed, staggered, and not from the pitch of the boat. Was she drugged or just hungry? She hadn't eaten since the chili in the trailer with Alex. She had no idea how long ago that had been.

Cautiously she tried the door handle, not wanting anyone on the other side to realize she was awake. The door was locked from the outside. Her heart dropped, but she shouldn't have expected otherwise.

Head spinning, she sat on the floor, hard. She only wanted to know where she was and if her son was on board. She glanced toward the windows that lined the room near the ceiling. Too narrow to crawl out, and even if she managed, what would she do next?

She needed to find out what hell she was sailing into.

Alex squeezed his eyes shut, then opened them again, trying to focus as he stared out at the bobbing boats in the marina. His head throbbed like a son of a bitch and every bump Julian had hit from the airport to the marina in the rented Jeep had only made it worse. Julian had instructed him to stay in the Jeep and though Alex rebelled, he knew now was the time to let others do the legwork. When it came to tracking Isabella down, he needed to be ready to go. Which meant he needed to rest while his team canvassed the area.

Saldana had screwed up at the airfield. He'd probably thought no one saw him split his crew, two men taking the Lear Jet, two more plus Saldana and an unconscious Isabella taking another SUV here to the marina.

Classic decoy. Good thing the mechanic working in a

nearby hangar had kept himself hidden or he might not be going home to his family this morning.

Unconscious. The mechanic's words had been "out of it", but Alex's mind ran with the possibilities. She was hurt, she was drugged, she was dead.

No, Alex couldn't believe that. Which meant that she was out there somewhere with a man who would hurt her, and she was defenseless.

His own helplessness hurt more than his damn shoulder. Now, if she was out at sea, how could he find her? She could be any damned where.

Julian pounded on the driver's side window, making Alex jolt, then swear as pain shot through him.

"What the fuck?" Alex demanded when his friend opened the door.

"We have the boat. Fifty-foot sailboat, registered to a Javier Bustos out of Belize. The plan they filed with the harbor master said they're heading back there, but it could be another decoy. Trouble is, they've got the GPS turned off. Could be anywhere."

The longer they took to find her, the more trouble she was in.

Please God, don't let him have taken her out to sea to dump her body. He had to see her again, had to hold her again, had to make sure she was safe before he turned away.

Isabella balanced on her toes on the narrow bunk and shoved at the latch on the window, but it was too high and she couldn't get leverage to push it open.

She whimpered in frustration, just stopping herself from pounding the frame with her fist.

Behind her the door handle turned and she whirled. Too

late to pretend she was still unconscious. Trapped. Her heart rabbited as she waited for the door to open.

The man who walked through was unfamiliar, and big. His eyes widened to see her standing on the cot. He stepped into the room and she hopped to the other side, keeping the bunk between herself and the stranger.

"Come with me."

The big man's voice didn't match his body, more high pitched than Isabella expected, as if she wasn't off balance enough. Her own voice sounded distant to her ears when she asked, "Where?"

"You are in no position to ask questions."

Even his tone was unexpected, not unkind. But when he approached, her trembling grew out of control so she had to grip the edge of the bunk to stay upright. Was he going to throw her overboard? The only question was if he'd shoot her first, or let her drown.

She wouldn't see her son again, or Alex. Bile bolted up her throat at the thought but she battled it back.

"I want my son." She wondered if he could understand her through her chattering teeth. "Is my son here?" If he was, whatever she had to do to pay for running from Santiago would be worth it, if she could only see him, touch him, hold him.

Something like sympathy flickered in the big man's eyes. "It's better if you come with me under your own power."

He was right. She struggled for self-control. To be forced to appear before Santiago would reveal her fear.

Still, he'd smell it on her, and feed on it.

She couldn't let her terror overwhelm her, though it threatened to pull her under. She had escaped from his compound, dropped over the side of a cliff, run through the jungle, attempted to seduce a guard, danced for information, run from men with automatic weapons and watched the man she loved shot as he tried to save her.

She could face Santiago.

Chills ran over her body as she moved past the big man into the narrow hall. Only one way to go, with a wall to her left. Her shoulders bumped the paneled walls with each sway of the boat, so how had this big guy made it through?

"Where?" she asked, wondering which of the doors hid her biggest nightmare.

If any held her deepest hope.

"Up the steps, and right."

The man didn't follow too close. He must not think she was much of a threat. Of course, he probably saw she could barely move because of her trembling. She managed the steps to the next level, and sunlight streamed over her as she reached the deck, warming her chilled skin. Every nerve screamed to turn left, jump over the rail, anything other than face the man who could destroy her.

She turned right and saw Santiago through the windows of the glassed-in room, leaning back in a leather chair, holding a highball glass containing God-knew-what. From experience, she knew it could improve his mood or increase his violence. Preparing herself for either outcome, she straightened her shoulders and reached for the door handle.

The room smelled of cigar smoke and power. She gagged on it. Santiago turned only his eyes to her, those light eyes that saw too much, that narrowed now in hatred. The animosity snagged her breath in her throat. What would he do to her before he killed her?

"Isabella. You look like hell."

She hadn't even thought of that. She, who had paid attention to every detail of her appearance when she lived with him, had not so much as looked in a mirror since before she and Alex ran to the Everglades. She resisted the urge to finger-comb her hair now, to show him any sign of vulnerability.

"Where is my son?"

Santiago's eyes widened a moment. "I do not remember you being so single-minded. You will see your son soon if you meet my conditions."

"What conditions?" But she knew and already mourned the fact that everything she'd had with Alex would be erased by the depraved acts Santiago would have her perform to see her son. Memories were all she had left of Alex now.

She might not live long enough to save Hector. Under Santiago's tutelage, he would become like his father. That thought weakened her knees more than fear for herself.

Santiago's eyes flicked toward the two men standing on either side of the doorway. Neither one was Pablo, thank God, but she knew them to be her punishment. The only thing, the only thing to keep her from wishing for death was the chance to see her son again. To ensure that she did, she had to fight. She tightened her jaw to hide its trembling.

"It doesn't matter what you do to me. The DEA has proof you killed Eric. Now you've killed an Army Ranger. They will never stop hunting you."

He inclined his head and swung his glass to the side, the gesture unconcerned. "They have to know where to find me. They've not been able to so far."

"They've never had greater motivation." She took a step closer, though her anger was quickly being swallowed by fear. "Know when they come for you that they found you because of me."

MJ Fredrick

She didn't see the glass tumbler swinging toward her until it was too late. It cracked against the side of her head hard enough to break. Pain sliced through her scalp and the upper part of her ear, and she dropped to her knees. The two men moved forward to grab her arms and yank them behind her. As her head swam, she prayed to fall into unconsciousness again. Even then, she knew Santiago would only make the men wait until she was awake and aware of every dirty thing they did to her.

She lifted her face to Santiago as warm blood trickled down the side of her throat. "I want to see my son," she repeated. Her choice had been made the moment she stepped out of the compound. "Whatever you want in payment, I'll do. Please. Is he here?"

Santiago leaned forward, forearms on his knees, a pleased expression on his face. "You will have plenty of time to pay for your mistakes before we get to Hector." He nodded to one of the men, who pushed her to her knees in front of Santiago.

Terror rose in her throat at the anticipation of what he wanted her to do. She couldn't bear the thought of taking his flaccid penis in her mouth. Already the scent of him gagged her.

He wrapped his fist around her hair and tugged hard, tearing strands loose from her scalp, and he kissed her hard, crushing her mouth, grinding her lips against her teeth, filling her with his filthy taste. She resisted the urge to bite down. She would do what he wanted until she saw her son.

He released her suddenly so that she slumped to the floor. "Where is your fight, Isabella?" He sat back and wiped his hand across his mouth. "Take her back to her room."

The man who'd pushed her to her knees now pulled her upright by her hair. She couldn't stop the squeal of pain, and she lifted her hands to relieve the pressure as she fought to get her feet under her.

"Give her time to think about all the things she knows I can do to her."

They'd drugged the food. Isabella realized it after a couple of bites of the mouthwatering grilled vegetables and fish. Now she felt woozy, and the scent of the food she'd set across the room made her stomach growl. To keep her mind off her hunger, she'd gone through the room, looking for a weapon. Yes, she'd said she'd do anything to get to her son again, but she hated the feeling of helplessness. If she knew she had something to protect herself, she would feel braver. The problem was every drawer was empty. But the action had at least given her something else to think about. She'd finally stopped shaking after her encounter with Santiago, but she refused to be broken until after she saw her child.

She could imagine Hector wriggling in her arms, anxious to get away from the kisses she longed to give him. So she would indulge him, playing the games he loved—hide and seek, treasure hunt and blowing bubbles. They'd sing and she'd tell him stories, and cuddle him every chance she got. She could almost smell him, and her heart swelled with longing.

The door handle turned and Isabella bolted off the bed, pressing her back to the window.

The same man from earlier came through the door and her trembling started anew. She resisted looking at the bed, where her punishment would no doubt come. Instead, the man left the door open and beckoned her.

"He wants to see you."

He glanced at the food on the tray and pressed his lips together, but said nothing, stepping to the side as she walked on wobbling legs toward the hall, forbidding her mind to go to the dark places Santiago could take her.

This time she was guided to another bedroom, stately, at the bow of the boat, windows looking over the horizon in what would be a beautiful view if she wasn't so terrified.

But she didn't see Santiago.

The door closed behind her and a fist struck the back of her head. Surprise and pain drove her to all fours. When she tried to push upright, to see past the fall of her hair, a hand pressed between her shoulder blades, holding her down. Another tugged at her jeans, and she felt the weight of a man's thighs against hers.

Her empty stomach roiled, and she choked her nausea back. She would endure this. She would. She just had to remember how to shut out the feelings she'd allowed to surface when she'd been with Alex.

The blow must have affected her hearing because she heard a buzzing. The weight left her body and she looked up to see Santiago move to a window, his attention drawn to the edge of the boat. Despite her dizziness, pain and fear, she scrambled to her feet.

A Coast Guard cutter approached, churning up water, destroying the peaceful view. Joy bubbled through her, but she banked it. So much had gone wrong, she was afraid to hope.

Until she saw Alex standing at the rail of the cutter, automatic weapon at the ready, suited up in a helmet and a bulletproof vest. His stance said they weren't getting out of here without going through his team of Rangers.

He was alive, standing strong. And he'd come for her.

Chapter Sixteen

Santiago shouted an alarm, pushing past her into the hall. He opened a closet in the hall and tossed guns to the three men who responded to his call. Terror squeezed Isabella's throat as the four men mounted the steps to the deck and she bolted after them, forgotten in the shadow of the new threat.

She reached the upper level as the men dropped to their bellies on the deck and leveled the weapons at the cutter.

"Guns!" she screamed in Alex's direction.

"Get down," he shouted back, and she lowered herself into the stairwell as gunfire broke out.

The glass wall in the room above her shattered under the hail of bullets, and shards sprinkled down on her. A strangled cry of pain burst from one of the men. At the same time, the boat lurched to the side, sending her rolling across the steps and bumping against the wall. Bullets hit the hull with horrible thunking sounds. Fear that they could penetrate all the way to the stairwell made her tremble. Would she hear the bullet that hit her?

Staying low, she crawled across the floor to see Santiago huddled in the corner while his men fought for him.

Coward.

She whipped around, grabbed a gun out of the back of the

fallen man's pants and pointed it at Santiago's face. Fear—and a touch of calculation—in his eyes snapped her muscles tight. Shaking, braced for the bullet that could kill her, she eased herself behind a chair, putting him between her and his men before she said, "Stop. Shooting. Now."

The men turned, guns raised, aimed at her. Then they saw her position, and knowing they risked hitting their boss, they lowered them.

Outside, gunfire still rattled.

"Alex, stop!" she screamed.

Santiago took advantage of her distraction and rose, pushing her gun hand high. She held onto the pistol—barely—and swung around with it, knocking him across the temple and onto the floor. Her finger trembled on the trigger and she could not think of one reason not to shoot him. Not one.

Alex was the first on the boat, sweeping his gun left to right. One man lay on the deck, unconscious. Another man lay inside what had been a sort of sun porch on the deck, now shattered. Beyond him, Isabella stood, a gun braced in both hands, pointing at the ground.

She looked up, her pretty face bruised, bloody and swollen, eyes terrified. Rage whipped through him. The urge to go to her, to sweep her into his arms, breathe her in, had him stepping forward, forgetting his training.

Before he touched her, he remembered the man on the floor, the gun she held.

"I have Santiago," she said.

She did too. The son of a bitch was bleeding from a head wound, all over the pretty white carpet. Alex wanted to draw more blood, maybe add some guts to it as well.

"You do that?"

She nodded.

He stopped himself from asking if Santiago had done the damage to her face. That would come later. "Good girl. Now come over here."

He reached out to her and she approached cautiously, then grasped his hand tightly. After giving her a brief, reassuring glance, he pulled her behind him, his attention on Santiago Saldana. He allowed himself a brief squeeze, pressing her against his side for a moment, feeling her heartbeat hammering, hearing a sharp intake of breath—pain?—before he pushed her away from Saldana. As badly as he wanted to hammer the son of a bitch into the carpet, he wanted Isabella safe.

So he left Saldana to Julian and Dave, who'd followed him, and escorted Isabella to the other boat. He lifted his fingers toward her bleeding temple, stopped himself before touching her and causing her more pain. His gaze flicked to the blood coating the side of her neck. He wanted Julian to look at her, to make sure the wound was only superficial. He didn't want her out of his sight.

"You need your head looked at."

Moments later, the prisoners were secured and she sagged on a bench in the Coast Guard cutter as Julian examined her scalp laceration. Her whole body drooped with exhaustion.

"I thought he'd take me to Hector. I wanted to see him. I thought I'd be holding him, Alex."

Alex hadn't released her, didn't want to stop touching her, and holding her hand was all he could allow in front of his men. He shouldn't even allow that but couldn't let her go.

All he had was words, and he was no good with them. "We'll find him, Bella."

She turned her gaze to him, eyes fierce in her battered, bloody, sad face. "Make him tell you. Make Santiago tell you where my son is."

Alex paced in the observation room as Captain Winters sat across the interrogation table from Santiago Saldana, the big fish they'd been trying to find for weeks. Because Saldana was here, Isabella was safe. She was safe. He didn't have to worry about her being at the hospital alone.

But Alex wanted to pound Saldana into the ground anyway. Likely that was the reason the captain wouldn't allow him into the interrogation room. Alex had promised Bella he'd stay and learn what he could about Hector. He just hadn't had the chance and the helplessness was making him restless.

He might feel better if Saldana was talking, but he remained stoically silent, hands folded on the table, eyes focused on the mirror, telegraphing some sort of message. Perhaps he thought Isabella was watching.

Agent Michaels entered the room, holding a folder. Ignoring Alex, he walked to the window and knocked to draw the captain's attention.

"What is that?" Alex asked, gesturing to the folder.

"More information we got off the drive the mistress brought us."

"Isabella Canales," Alex corrected. He knew what she'd been, could live with it, but he didn't want others thinking of her like that. Like he had. Judging her. "She risked her life to get the drive from Saldana'a office and bring it to us."

Agent Michaels shot him a glance. "Right. It should come in handy now. This stuff should get a rise out of him."

"He's waiting for his lawyer."

"Lawyer's been held up at security." Michaels' grin was quick. "Too bad."

"Any information in there that might tell us where he stashed the kid?"

Michaels turned to face him full-on now. "You're still worried about that?"

"She wants her kid back. The least you can give her in exchange for all that." He nodded to the stack of papers in the folder.

Michaels flipped open the folder, thumbed through the pages. "I think there were some real estate records in here, other houses Saldana owns. Poor kid doesn't stand a chance, though, with either parent. You gotta wonder if the state will let her keep him. Here you go. Three more properties Saldana owns, none in the US. He probably stashed the kid in one of those places."

Alex trembled with the desire to slam the agent into the wall for saying those things about Isabella, but hadn't he thought the same? He hated himself for having made those judgments about her.

But he pushed the desire aside, thinking of the joy he'd bring Isabella when he told her he'd found Hector. He could already imagine the way her eyes would shine. He grabbed the folder from Michaels, jotted the information down on a scrap of paper and slapped the manila folder against Michaels' chest.

"For the record," he said. "She's the strongest, bravest woman I've known. You keep that asshole in here so he doesn't touch her again."

Isabella was numb on the flight to Belize. Alex had been so excited when he'd burst into her hotel room, scaring the hell out of her, and had gotten surly when she didn't respond the way he thought she would. Didn't he realize how afraid she was to hope that she'd find her son? She'd been crushed so many times.

So she'd sat silently while he made arrangements for a friend of a friend to fly them down immediately. He'd lost his temper when she insisted she needed a new dress for the occasion. The only way she'd convinced him to stop at a department store was because she didn't even have shoes. He didn't understand that everything had to be perfect when she saw her son again.

She tightened her grip on the toy puppy Alex had grabbed while she changed into the red knit dress. That he'd thought of her son, of something to please him, made her heart swell with more emotion she had to squash. One step at a time.

She caught her reflection in the plane's window. She hadn't been able to do anything about the bruises and swelling on her face, and had been painfully aware of the stares she and Alex had received. That only made his mood worse, and he hadn't said much on the flight so far.

Now the plane was circling, and Isabella's thoughts right along with it. *Please, God, let him be here. Please, God, let me hold him. Please, God, let this be over, even if it means saying goodbye to Alex.*

He was watching her now, gauging her reaction, she supposed. Unable to meet whatever expectations he might have of her, she turned and looked out the window at the green land, the blue water, her son's favorite colors. She hummed softly to herself, the Black Eyed Peas song she'd altered to teach her son his colors, as the plane circled, then touched down on a tiny airfield near the coast.

An SUV waited for them. Alex took her arm as he guided her toward it, casting a disgusted glance at her new heels.

"Didn't you learn anything this past week?"

"I learned I can run barefoot," she retorted, then opened her bag to show him the Keds she'd picked up. "I learned how to be prepared."

His grin surprised her as he opened the passenger door for her. "I wonder if I'll ever figure you the hell out."

A little pop of joy burst in her chest. Did that mean he was going to stick around once this was over? No, no. One step at a time.

She gripped the armrest in the SUV as Alex guided it over rough roads, then, using the GPS as a guide, up a winding road, trees thick on both sides. Isabella's heart hammered in anticipation and fear. On the plane, Alex had assured her getting Hector out of the compound wouldn't be difficult. He carried paperwork that verified her claim of parenthood and more that showed Santiago was in jail, and would be for a long time. Still, she'd feel more secure if the Rangers had come with them.

The road made a final turn, revealing an Italian-style mansion overlooking the Caribbean. The stucco walls gleamed in the sunlight, the arched windows reflected it. The house itself was surrounded by bougainvillea and hibiscus, thriving in the tropical climate. A wall matching the house ran the length of the yard, and a moment passed before Isabella found the wrought-iron gate, hidden from the road.

This compound wasn't hiding. It was huge and looming and actually pretty. Why couldn't Santiago have kept her here?

She sat forward in her seat, her hand on the door handle, her breath caught in her chest. Was that—oh, God. She shoved the door open before Alex stopped, stumbled a bit in the gravel of the road, scuffing her new shoes but not caring as she ran to the gate and curled her fingers around it, looking through the scrolled iron bars at the dark-haired child playing on a manicured lawn. Giggles carried on the breeze from the ocean below, and a word. "Mama!"

Her heart squeezed when she realized her son hadn't seen her. He was running toward a brunette woman who bent to scoop him up and lifted him high. She recognized Carmen. So she wasn't in Florida after all. The air echoed with squeals of delight.

Isabella's knees sagged and she would have dropped to the ground, but suddenly Alex was beside her, his arm around her, holding her up.

"I'm sorry, Bella. I'm sorry," he said against her temple. "Maybe one of the other houses—"

"He called her 'Mama'," she choked, barely managing the words that were being strangled by tears she refused to release.

He drew back sharply. "It's him?"

She nodded, her grip so tight on the gate that the scrolls dug into her palms. Her son, and she'd be damned if she let him call another woman "Mama" after what she'd gone through to get him. She drew away from Alex and rose onto her toes.

"*Mijo*," she called through the gate, then louder. "*Mijo.*"

Carmen straightened and turned toward the gate. Her spine snapped straight when she saw Isabella. Hector wriggled in her arms, twisting. She saw recognition light his eyes, and he held his arms out to her with a sharp cry of "Mama".

Isabella rattled the gate, needing to get to him, ready to climb over it, ready to take a swipe at Alex when he pushed her back from it. But then he bent over the lock and popped it open, swinging the gate wide. Joy pouring through her, Isabella raced into the yard.

She dropped to her knees and flung her arms wide, and

Hector, her baby, the love of her life, threw himself against her, calling, "Mama, Mama," over and over. She folded her arms around him, folded her body over his. She had her son and no one was going to get him away from her again. Tears blurred her vision of the boy as she pressed kisses all over his sweet face, as she breathed in the scent of him, little-boy sweat under baby shampoo. This had to be real, if she could smell him, right?

She didn't want to let go of her son, checking him to make sure he was whole. His chubby little arms were tight around her neck, pulling her hair, and his body pressed into her cracked ribs, but she was so glad, so relieved he hadn't forgotten her.

She looked up to see Alex, blurry through her tears, watching her. "Thank you," she managed through the lump in her throat.

He didn't say anything, of course, only took her elbow and lifted her up, Hector and all. He pulled her against his side, just for a minute, long enough for her to feel the sigh of relief from him.

Cradling her baby in her arms, she turned to Carmen. Tension returned in full force when she met the eyes of the woman who served Santiago. Beyond her, two men built like linebackers stepped out of the house. But Alex betrayed no alarm. He released her to approach them, leaving her alone with her son and Carmen. She battled back the resentment she felt, for the time this woman had spent with her child that she hadn't. For just a moment, she wanted to know every detail of the past few months, everything she'd missed in her son's life. But to indulge in that meant a delay in getting home, in getting back to normal. She didn't want to wait for that a moment longer.

With a protective hand over the back of Hector's head, she spoke. "Santiago is in jail. This is over. I'm taking him home."

Carmen frowned, then nodded, her gaze focusing on Hector. "He cried for you. For months, he cried for you."

"I'm here now. Santiago can't hurt us anymore. You can't hurt us anymore."

"I didn't do it to hurt you."

Just to get in Santiago's good graces. Isabella understood. "That doesn't make it better."

Carmen's mouth tightened. "Do you want his things?"

Isabella looked toward the house. Things bought with Santiago's money. "No." She tightened her grip on Hector's bottom, adjusting him in her arms. Funny how she'd forgotten how heavy such a slight weight could get after a few minutes. "No, I'll take care of him from now on."

Alex strode across the yard toward her, matter of factly. "Let's go. They have Santiago's lawyer's number if they need to verify anything." But his body language told her they should go before more questions were raised.

She buckled Hector into the built-in car seat in the back of the SUV and sat beside him, unwilling to let him out of her sight for the drive back to the airport. She wanted to talk to him, have him tell her about the time she'd lost. More than once she caught Alex watching them in the rearview mirror, but his expression was odd, a mixture of pride and longing, she thought. Longing for what, though?

The flight to Florida was long, but she didn't care, only measured her baby's breathing, smoothed his dark hair, felt his heartbeat. She'd never felt a joy, a relief, this strong since the day he was born. Like then, this moment was worth everything she'd endured to get here.

Her cheek still pressed against Hector's head, she turned to smile at Alex, who almost—almost—smiled in return.

Isabella watched Alex through her lashes as they sat in a booth at the cozy little diner down the street from the Miami airport. They'd been detained at the airport the better part of the night as she'd tried to prove Hector was her son. She'd told the authorities that his birth certificate had been lost in a fire, but they hadn't been inclined to believe her. Her battered face likely did nothing to advance her cause. It wasn't until Alex called in a few favors from his friends at the DEA that they released her. Agent Michaels faxed over documentation that had been on the thumb drive, a scanned birth certificate and several doctor reports, including a DNA test Isabella didn't even know Santiago had ordered. He must have doubted the child was his.

But now she thanked him for it, because there was no question about her child's parentage. She could take him home without worrying someone would take him away again.

Alex to the rescue again.

He hadn't flinched when she ordered the biggest breakfast on the menu. He even prodded Hector into ordering milk and orange juice, though that much liquid in such a small bladder could only cause delays. She hated that she felt nervous, waiting for Hector's incessant chatter to get on Alex's nerves. Alex wasn't used to children, after all, and Hector had slept well and was now wide-awake.

Santiago had hated spending any extended period of time with Hector because he was so noisy. Santiago was accustomed to everyone doing what he wanted, not taking into account Hector was only a child.

So she waited for Alex to lose his temper. So far, though, he only watched the child warily.

She wanted to ask him what this all meant, that he was still here with her, but every time she met his gaze, his was guarded. She didn't know how to get past that.

"We're heading to Orlando after this," he told her when the waitress came to clear the plates.

"Why?" She wiped absently at Hector's mouth, as if she hadn't been out of practice for four months.

He flicked a glance at Hector. "I've been given forty-eight hours of leave and we're going to Disney World." He mouthed the last two words so the boy wouldn't hear.

An emotion she was afraid to name bubbled up so that she had to push the words out. "You don't have to do that. I'm already happier than I've ever been."

He folded his napkin and tossed it on the table, not looking at her. "I keep my word, Bella."

What did that mean? She knew that. He'd said he'd protect her and he had. He said he'd get her son back and he had. The Disney World promise—that had just been to get her through it, right?

Or not.

So they drove to Orlando. Alex got them a room with two double beds on the resort, and after a trip to Walmart to replenish their supplies, courtesy of the US Army this time, Isabella gave her son a bubble bath. The splashing and giggling held Alex's attention, a foreign sound, and he resisted the urge to go watch. This was their time together and they needed to be alone, no matter how much Alex ached to be a part of it.

Once the kid came barreling out of the bathroom, wrapped only in a towel to bounce on the bed, Alex rose to walk to the bathroom. They hadn't had much time to talk, especially for him to scold her, not when she'd been hurt, then anxious, then so happy. Now her emotions had evened out, and it was time. He braced his hands in the doorway and she beamed up at him, truly glowed.

"You scared the hell out of me when you went with Danes, you know."

She dropped her gaze and he cursed himself for making her smile dim.

"I know. I'm sorry. I thought—you trusted him. When I saw him pull up, I thought he'd come to tell us about Hector."

"I did trust him," he admitted. "I was stupid."

The smile disappeared altogether now. Good. She got that he didn't trust anyone, not even her.

"But you came after me." She looked up at him with adoration in those big brown eyes.

"I did," he agreed, wanting to turn away. But he was no coward. "You were my responsibility. I was supposed to keep you safe."

Hurt flashed in her eyes. "That's not all I am to you, Alex. If it was, you would have said goodbye to us at the airport instead of bringing us back to Orlando."

"I'm your protector. With Santiago behind bars, you don't need me." As soon as the words left his mouth, he realized instead of sounding cruel to push her away, he sounded needy.

She heard it too, damn her, and stood to move closer, letting the sopping towels fall into the tub. Her fingers were cool and wet as she touched his cheek.

"I need you. I love you, Alex."

He took a step back and looked away sharply at her words. "You don't. You don't know anything about me other than I saved your life and brought you your son."

She laughed. "That's a lot to know." She came nearer. "You stood by me through all of this. You risked everything to help me. You risked your career, the respect of everyone around you to help me. You killed someone who meant something to you to help me. You're my hero."

He turned to her then. "I'm not a hero all the time, Bella."

"No?" She smiled. "When aren't you?"

"When I used to sell drugs."

She blinked, surprised, and let her hand fall away. "You did?" She glanced past him to her son, who was happily engrossed in a SpongeBob cartoon Alex had turned on. He waited for her to return her attention to him. He needed to see her reaction.

He needed to push her and her child away.

"I was a drug mule for five years."

"You—were?"

Doubt and confusion shadowed her eyes. There, if he looked close, was a bit of disgust. He focused on that.

"Where?" she asked.

"In Houston. For my mom."

"For your mom?" Her brow furrowed. "I thought you were adopted."

"When I was fourteen."

The frown lines relaxed. "You were a mule for your real mom?"

"Yeah."

He watched her reason it out.

"So you were—nine when you started?"

"More like six. I was in the system awhile before the Shepards got me."

"Oh, Alex." She laughed again, in relief, and wrapped her arms around his neck. "You were just a baby. You didn't know what you were doing. You thought you were helping your mom."

He reached up to loosen her arms, but she wouldn't let go. He scowled, frustrated. He had to allow her to see his dark side, a side only the Shepards understood. He'd never wanted anyone else to know. Why he needed her to, well, he wasn't sure. "I helped kill my mom. She died running from the cops when I was eleven, in a car rollover. I was in the backseat."

"Alex." Her voice was soft, curling around him as she curved her palms over the back of his head and looked into his eyes. "How terrible for you."

This time he managed to get away from her, wanting some distance. "It was the best thing to ever happen to me." He gauged her reaction to his statement. Horror, as he expected. As any loving mother would feel. "She was a whore, Bella. She sold herself, sold me, for drugs."

He watched understanding sink in and her generous lips thinned.

"That's why you held me so far away. You thought I was like her?"

He braced his hands against the dresser behind him. "Consider my frame of reference here."

She twisted the damp towel around her arms. "But now you know differently."

It was almost a question, with a hint of hope. He sucked in a breath, knowing what she wanted to hear. He wanted to say the words but knew what she would want if he said them.

Something he couldn't give. Something he didn't deserve.

He'd already made too much of taking them to Disney World. That was a treat for a family, and while he'd enjoy it, he'd known all the while that he'd be walking away and never see either of them again.

"I know you're strong, and you love that kid more than anything. I know who you are."

"But you can't love me because of who I was."

The pain was sharp in her voice and he moved forward, catching her wrists to force her to look at him. He waited for the fear to flash in her eyes, after what she'd endured, but there was none. Wonder filled him at that. She wasn't afraid of him. That didn't make what he had to say any easier.

"Because of who I was, Bella."

She sucked in a breath. "If you can't forgive yourself for your past, can't see the man you've become, then you'll never forgive me for mine."

He opened his mouth, wanting to ease her pain as much as he'd wanted to return her son to her, all the while worried it was beyond his power. This was just as far beyond his power. It was best to let her believe he thought that.

"Mama?"

She didn't go to her son right away, just looked at Alex, hoping. When he didn't say anything, she scooped up her naked boy, cuddling him close, his chubby little arms going around her neck, confident that she'd be there for him always.

Christ, he wouldn't wimp out here and cry.

"We're both tired," she said in a soft voice, then jiggled her son in her arms. "We have a big exciting day tomorrow. I've never been to Disney World, either."

She smiled at her son and the whole room brightened, everything within him brightened, but he retreated into his own shadows. Safer for everyone there, as it had always been.

"Let's get you dressed," she murmured to her son, easing

past Alex into the main room.

Alex stood perfectly still, but the scent of her still filled him with longing.

Disney World was amazing, everything she could have dreamed of and more. They were fortunate they accompanied a three-year-old, since with their injuries they couldn't handle the more exhilarating rides. Anyway, Isabella had had her fill of excitement.

Alex flashed her a grin when they passed the Tower of Terror and heard the piercing screams as the riders dropped in a free fall.

"Sounds like you on the side of that cliff," he teased.

Hector was in heaven, and Alex indulged him with sweets and souvenirs. Isabella had never seen the man so relaxed. He even chuckled a few times, a sound she'd never heard.

She never thought she'd be so in love with a man under such control.

She'd told him she loved him, and he hadn't said anything. Of course she didn't want him to say it if he didn't mean it— she'd heard it from men who'd tried to charm her to get their way with her. But if Alex said them, that meant she was the one for him. She longed for that more than she could say.

What a childhood he'd had—if she could call it a childhood. He would hate knowing she pitied him, hate knowing she'd give anything to go back to fix it for him.

But he'd had a good life with his foster parents. He knew what it was like to be part of a family. Did the responsibility scare him? Maybe it did—though she'd never seen him scared of anything. Still, she came complete with a child.

She didn't think that was Alex's issue. He was great with

Hector. Hector was shy—he hadn't known many men in his young life—but Alex was gentle and easy with him, learning how to interact with the child as the child learned how to interact with the man. Someday he would be a great dad.

Just not for her child.

That would be an unacceptable loss for all of them.

God, her feelings for him were so complicated. He made her feel safe, he challenged her, she admired his courage. She desired him.

He took her hand and led her toward the Dumbo ride.

"Oh, if you're going on that, I need a camera," she laughed.

"I'll buy you anything," he said, walking backwards, his fingers threaded through hers. "Except that."

Alex carried the sleeping boy to the shuttle that would take them to their hotel, careful to keep his weight off the bruised ribs. Isabella walked beside him, dragging, laden with stuffed animals, Mickey ears, a giant lollypop—hers, not Hector's. Even the pert little ponytail she'd flipped around all day was drooping. He reached back for her free hand and found it easily, as he had all day. He shoved aside the longing that accompanied the gesture.

The same longing he saw in her eyes whenever he looked at her.

So easy to crush that hope. Even if he decided to give in, even if he promised when he came back from his next assignment that they would give this a shot, how long would it last? A month? A year? Who would lose interest first? They both might be too stubborn to admit defeat, or they might fight it out, all the while knowing they'd be better off apart.

No. Best to end it tonight, go back with his team tomorrow,

back on assignment, away from her. She could find happiness on her own. She didn't need his protection anymore.

He stepped onto the too-bright shuttle, shielding Hector's eyes, sitting on one of the hard plastic seats gingerly so he wouldn't wake the boy. Isabella dropped to the seat beside him and let her head fall to his shoulder.

"Good day," she murmured.

He squeezed her hand as the shuttle lurched forward. "Yeah."

"What time do you leave tomorrow?"

"I have to report at five."

"God, Alex, that's in seven hours. I won't be able to move in seven hours." She tucked her other arm through his and snuggled closer.

"Can't carry both of you," he said, smiling down at her.

"Won't sleep," she promised drowsily.

The warmth of her, the weight of the boy, all of it felt right. Everything he'd wanted with Rebecca. A family. If he'd been willing to risk his heart for Rebecca, why couldn't he do it for Isabella? She was stronger, she was in love with him, she didn't back away, even knowing what she did about him, something he would have always had to hide from Rebecca.

He could hurt her. He hadn't worried about that so much with Rebecca, he'd been so concerned with taking care of her. But with Isabella, it would be worse.

No. He was walking away in the morning. For good.

They reached the stop at the hotel, and he stood, helped Isabella to her feet. A woman across the aisle, older, maybe the age of his foster mom, reached out to him.

"You have a lovely family," she murmured.

He smiled tightly despite the pinch in his chest, nodded,

235

and walked off.

"Bella. I'm going." Alex crouched by her bed and stroked her hair back from her face, studied her beauty in the dim light of the bedside lamp. He'd resisted crawling into bed with her the past two nights, not to make love to her, but just to hold her, feel her warmth, her trust, even as she slept.

And now he was walking away.

She blinked awake and rolled toward him. "Already? Alex." She reached out to touch his shirt, frowned when she encountered his camouflage shirt.

"I'm sorry." About so much.

Her eyes sharpened. She understood. Still, she asked, "When will we see you again?"

"You don't need me anymore, Bella."

"But I want you."

He didn't answer that, couldn't, just let the soft words roll through him. Instead, he pushed back from the bed, not rising yet. "Take care of yourself and the little guy. The room is paid for another night, and there's some cash—"

"We'll be fine. We're—going home after this. Let Hector meet his grandparents."

"Good. That's good." He glanced at the clock. He should have left fifteen minutes ago, but he was dragging, and he knew the reason why.

She took his hand. "Be careful, Alex."

"I will."

"Thank you."

He rose then and smirked. "You're welcome."

She sat as he made his way across the room to the door,

following his progress with her eyes. He needed to turn away. He couldn't do this, say goodbye.

"I love you," she said again when he opened the door.

He took a deep breath before he could take the last step out. "Goodbye, Bella."

You can go home again. Isabella drove her rental car around the mountains, through El Paso, over the state line and into Las Cruces. In the backseat, secure in his child seat, Hector alternately flipped through his books and looked at the scenery.

Las Cruces was a beautiful little town at the foot of the Organ Mountains on the New Mexico side, and she caught her breath to see the place for the first time in six years.

Just like she'd caught her breath to hear her mama's voice when she'd called from Orlando.

Was it okay if she came home for a little while? Did they want to meet their grandson?

She might never be sure if Hector was her ticket home. If her parents would be just as happy to see her, alone.

She turned and turned and turned again, her body remembering the way home. There it was, the little ranch house where she'd grown up, restless and unappreciative. It had never looked so beautiful, with its new coat of sand-colored paint, neatly trimmed grass, flowers on the porch.

Everything blurred and she pried her fingers from the steering wheel and turned to look at Hector with a smile. "Do you want to go meet your grandparents?"

Then they were there, running out to the car, pulling her out, hugging her, pulling Hector out, staring at him, stroking him, laughing, crying, never letting go of Isabella.

She knew she'd have to talk to them, knew she'd have to make up for disappearing six years ago. But for now, she was home.

Alex set the bottle of beer on the table in front of his father, drank from his own before sitting.

"Don't tell your mother," Tim Shepard said, opening the bottle.

"Why does she keep it if you can't drink it?"

"Hoping you'll come home." He took a long drink, one eye on the door.

"I come home enough."

His father nodded. "More than most men your age. Something different, this time, though."

Alex kept his gaze on the beer. "What do you mean?"

"You're tense, restless. Like you were when you came to us. Something go wrong on this last mission?"

Alex's heart jumped just a little. He didn't lie to his father. "No, sir. Not this one."

His father leaned back. "The one before. The one with the girl and her child."

"Yeah." Alex shoved the beer away, watched it slide in the condensation, then scraped one hand down his face. "I can't get her out of my head. Even on the last mission, Cervantes had to call me on it."

"You love her?"

Alex snorted. "I thought I loved Rebecca, look how that ended up."

"So how is this different?"

Alex studied the label of his beer, saw Bella's face. "Isabella is strong, so fucking strong—"

"Alex."

His face heated when his father chided him for his language, and he apologized for the slip. "I started off thinking she was like my—real mother, you know, that she was only after money and pleasure, no matter what the cost. I kept telling myself that even after I knew it wasn't true, because I wanted her so bad, and I thought—" He shook his head. "I thought that could hold me off. But she's amazing and tough and there's this light in her, especially when she's with her son, Hector. I start thinking about it—can I be a good dad to someone that little? I mean, I didn't have a dad till I was older. But he'd have good schools on base. Living on base might be hard for Bella, she can be a little hellion, but I think she'll adjust."

"Son." His father leaned close, eyebrows lifted. "You sound like—"

"Yes, sir, but how do I know it's real?" He pushed to his feet. "How can I tell it's love and not lust and not obsession? If I go to her and tell her that I love her, what guarantee do I have that it will last? I mean, she won't tell me no, she said she loved me, but how can I be sure she knows what it means? Neither of us have had the best judgment when it comes to that."

His father sat back with a sigh and tasted his beer. "The fact that you're worried about it assures me a little. The idea that you're planning for a future."

Alex looked over. "Yeah?"

"If it was lust, you'd be thinking about how long before you got tired of her. If it was obsession, you wouldn't be here asking me if it was the right thing. You already have the answer, Alex. I

239

know it's hard for you to trust your feelings, but you need to."

"I love her?"

His father chuckled. "Way to sound convinced, my boy."

Alex dropped against the back of his chair with a grin. "I love her." He stood up and threw his arms up into the air. "I love her!"

His mother came out on the porch, drawn by the commotion. Alex snatched her up and spun her around.

"I love her."

His mother swatted him with the dishtowel. "Then go tell her, you dummy."

Alex stood at the edge of the sidewalk, watching the young woman in the shorts and tank top splashing her son in the plastic kiddie pool, jumping in and kicking the water up, jumping out again when he returned a wave of water.

She looked so happy. Did he have any right walking back into her life and saying, "Hey, look, I was wrong, you were right, I love you, let's give this a shot?" He was asking a lot of her, to move to North Carolina with him, so she could be there for him between missions.

Goddamn, he never used to be this indecisive. But one decision had never meant more.

Before he could second-guess himself back to the car, she looked up and saw him.

Even from this distance, he saw the question in her eyes. What did this mean, him turning up here? He could see the hope. God, he loved her hope, the belief that she'd find her son, the trust that he'd stand by her side.

He wanted to honor that trust, live with that hope. He wanted her light to chase all his shadows away.

And then she was running toward him, long brown legs eating up the ground. She flung her arms around him, holding tight, her legs flying off the ground as he wrapped his arms around her. She raised her head, looked into his eyes, saw something there, because she kissed him like she'd been starving for him, hard and hot and open mouthed.

Something struck his leg, attached to it, soaking his neatly pressed slacks. Hector. He loosened his hold on Isabella enough to look down at the grinning toddler, felt himself grinning in response.

From a distance he heard a woman calling. The light in Bella's eyes changed to mischief and she peeled herself off him, but didn't let go, pressed herself to his side, clinging to his arm to show he didn't have a chance of escape.

He followed her gaze to the house, where a woman with Isabella's eyes stood, hands together, watching.

"Are you up for meeting my mama?" she asked, but started leading him down the sidewalk before he could answer.

Dinner was a cheerful affair, and if he hadn't been adopted by the Shepards, he would never have known how to deal. Bella's dad watched him warily, her mom kept trying to feed him, Hector clamored for his attention, and all the while Bella smiled, knowledge in her eyes.

He wished he knew what she did.

After dinner, her mother chased them outside and they sat on the bench of a brand-new swing set.

"He's not spoiled or anything," Alex said, trailing his finger along the chain of the swing as she curled up beside him. She hadn't let go of him yet, as if she was afraid he'd disappear or run away. Something in him flinched. He was here to ask her to come to North Carolina with him. How could he take her away from the family she'd just rediscovered?

"Neither of us are." She rested her head on her shoulder and sighed. "You're probably wondering why I left."

"Yeah, a bit."

"My family is great, but not what I'd call adventurous. I wanted adventure."

"Now you've had it."

She laughed. "More than my share."

"So you're ready to settle down."

The catch in her breath told him she caught his meaning.

"Depends on what kind of settling down you're thinking of."

He shifted so he could look at her, and regretted that the movement dislodged her head from his shoulder. "The kind where you come to North Carolina and learn how to be a soldier's wife."

Her eyes filled with tears, but she smiled. "That doesn't really sound like settling down."

His lips twitched. "No, it's just another kind of adventure, come to think about it."

"A soldier's wife," she repeated. "Are you sure, Alex, after everything you know about me?"

"This is what I know about you." He cupped her face in his palms. "You're passionate and loyal and loving. There's a light inside you I can't stand to be away from. Maybe I'm selfish in wanting you with me, but—"

She covered his hand with hers. "No. Not selfish."

He reached into his pocket for the square box that had been riding on his hip for the past few hours. He opened it with fumbling fingers and presented it to her. "I love you, Bella. I want you to know you're not taking all the risk here."

"I know all about risks, good and bad," she murmured, looking from the ring to his face, her eyes just as bright as the diamond. "You're a risk I'm willing to take."

About the Author

MJ Fredrick knows about chasing dreams. Twelve years after she completed her first novel, she signed her first publishing contract. Now she divides her days between teaching 4th grade students how to write and diving into her own writing, traveling everywhere in her mind, from Belize to Honduras to Africa to the past.

To learn more about MJ, please visit www.mjfredrick.com or www.marywritesromance.blogspot.com. You can email her at mjfredrick13@gmail.com or join her Yahoo group at http://groups.yahoo.com/group/mjfredrick. She's also on Facebook and Twitter under MJFredrick.

When past and present meet, secrets lie beneath the surface.

Beneath the Surface
© 2009 M.J. Fredrick

In retrospect, perhaps archaeologist Mallory Reeves shouldn't have delivered the divorce papers to her estranged husband mere weeks before her marriage to another man. She knew seeing Adrian again would stir up memories, but she didn't expect so many of them to be good, not after the mess they both made three years ago.

She also didn't expect to want to stay at the dig site on the Yucatan Peninsula. But the lure of the ancient ship and, yes, her sexy ex provide more of a draw than the white picket fence she thought she wanted.

Marine archaeologist Adrian Reeves has good reason to trust no one. His former partner—and *former* best friend—made off with his last archaeological find. And his wife left him, frustrated by his obsession for professional revenge.

Now both Mallory and his nemesis have returned, and it can't be an accident that they've turned up in the middle of the most important excavation of his career. Seeing her again unearths old pain—and rekindles never-forgotten desire. Now he has to decide if he can trust Mallory again. More importantly, if he can trust himself with her.

Warning: Smokin' hot archaeologists, painful memories, breathtaking underwater scenes and a passion that won't die.

Available now in ebook and print from Samhain Publishing.

Blood ties run deepest—and deadliest.

Proof of Life
© *2009 Misty Evans*
Super Agent Series, book 3

No matter how many times he patches the holes in the wall, CIA Deputy Director Michael Stone can't forget the night a terrorist took him hostage in his own home. Or the mistakes that transformed him into an overwhelming force to keep his country safe. And now that his niece, the daughter of the Republican candidate for President, has been kidnapped just days from the election, Michael vows to do whatever it takes to get her back.

Dr. Brigit Kent, a consultant for the Department of Homeland Security, knows this particular kidnapper well. Exposing him, however, will reveal her sister's secret ties to a terrorist group. The only way to keep her sister safe is to blackmail the sexy, rock-solid deputy director. A move that puts her directly in his line of fire.

Brigit is undeniably beautiful, brilliant, cunning. But is she friend or foe? The answer to that question could break Michael's personal code of honor—and his heart.

Warning: Bullets and blackmail, good luck and laughter. Surprises and secrets and love ever after...

Available now in ebook and print from Samhain Publishing.

hot stuff

Discover Samhain!

THE HOTTEST NEW PUBLISHER ON THE PLANET

Romance, fantasy, mystery, thriller, mainstream and more—Samhain has more selection, hotter authors, and everything's available in ebook.

Pick your favorite, sit back, and enjoy the ride! Hot stuff indeed.

GREAT
cheap
fun

Discover eBooks!

THE FASTEST WAY TO GET THE HOTTEST NAMES

Get your favorite authors on your favorite reader, long before they're
out in print! Ebooks from Samhain go wherever you go, and work with
whatever you carry—Palm, PDF, Mobi, and more.

Samhain
publishing LTD

WWW.SAMHAINPUBLISHING.COM

Lightning Source UK Ltd.
Milton Keynes UK
07 November 2010

162545UK00001B/24/P